MY NAME IS NOBODY

Books by
Maureen Wartski

The Lake Is On Fire
A Long Way from Home
A Boat to Nowhere
My Brother is Special

MY NAME IS NOBODY

Maureen Crane Wartski

Walker and Company
New York

First published in the United States of America in 1988 by the Walker Publishing Company, Inc.

Published simultaneously in Canada by Thomas Allen and Son, Canada, Limited, Markham, Ontario.

Library of Congress Cataloging-in-Publication Data

Wartski, Maureen Crane, 1940–
My name is nobody.

Summary: A desperate teenager on the brink of suicide is rescued by a retired policeman who gives the boy a home and an appreciation for life.
[1. Suicide—Fiction. 2. Friendship—Fiction]
I. Title.
PZ7.W2582Myn 1988 [Fic] 87-21574
ISBN 0-8027-6770-2
ISBN 0-8027-6771-0 (lib. bdg.)

Printed in the United States of America

10 9 8 7 6 5 4 3 2 1

To Jo Crane and to Maximilian,
with my love.

ACKNOWLEDGEMENTS

My thanks to Lynne Allen, Special-Needs Teacher at Sharon High School; Marilyn Scott, MSW; and sailing consultants Stanley and Scott Rubinstein and Bert Wartski.

MY NAME IS NOBODY

CHAPTER 1

I couldn't see the ground.

Maybe fog from Boston Harbor. Maybe night wind, making my eyes water. It didn't matter. I took a step forward.

"Hey—lookit, a jumper on the roof!"

I stood on the edge. Excited voices ballooned up from below.

"He's going to jump!"

Night wind smacked me. Cold—I was so cold. And empty. All I had to do was to move my feet over the edge. All the emptiness would go away.

"Do it!" someone shouted. "Why don't you jump!"

Do it, Rob. In my aching head an old tune replayed. *You're a lousy chicken,* Pa's voice sneered. *Call yourself my son? You can't even kill yourself right. What are you waiting for?*

I thought about the last rotten months. Eating garbage. Sleeping in doorways. Hassled. Starved. Beaten. Running. So lonely—like constant pain. What could be worse?

I shuffled one foot forward.

"Boy—stop right there. Don't do it."

The new voice came from behind me. Surprise should have sent me plunging. Instead, it pulled me back. Someone was on the roof near me—maybe fifty feet away. I couldn't see a face, but the voice was raspy, deep. A man's voice. I could see a clump of white hair blowing in the cruel wind.

"Don't you come near me!" I screamed.

"I'm not going to do anything without your say-so." A pause. "I just want to make sure you know what you're doing, son. If you step off this roof, you'll die and be dead forever."

The crowd below was getting restless. "Isn't he going to do it?" a woman demanded.

"Don't listen," the man behind me said. "You want to be a night's entertainment for them, huh? Want to splatter your guts all over the pavement to please them?"

I wouldn't listen. But just as I pushed my foot forward, he said, "My name is Kurt Doyle. Who are you, boy?"

"Nobody," I snapped. "Go away."

"I live in Laysner on the Cape. That's Cape Cod. Ever been that way? Nice place to live in, beautiful this time of year. When summer comes, it gets too busy, but right now in the spring it's special, all right. The ocean turns a different color by the hour, and you can take your boat and sail right into the Atlantic Ocean through the bottleneck. You ever done any sailing?"

My lip was raw where I'd been chewing it. Sailing?

I could have cried. Sure, right, I've sailed through life. It's been a barrel of laughs. "Go *away*!" I pleaded.

He paid no attention. "Just you and the water," he said. "The sky can look like a mackerel's back or be so blue it hurts your eyes. I'd like to take you home with me and show you how good it can all be. Just step away from the edge and take my hand."

I felt dizzy. And sick. Only one way to stop feeling this way . . .

"Death will hurt, son," he was telling me. "The wind will sear your lungs when you step into space. The pavement will hit you hard. You won't have time to black out before you come down on it."

"Shut up!" I screamed, "I'm doing it." But I couldn't move.

"Tell you what you are going to do. You are going to turn away from the edge of the roof and take my hand."

He had inched nearer to me. I could make him out, square, chunky body, white hair blowing.

"You think you've got no place to go, but you do. You'll come home with me." His voice had turned urgent. "I don't know what's happening in your life, but I want to help. I care what happens to you. I'll stand by you."

I hesitated. Somebody in the crowd below began to boo. "He's chickening out."

I whipped around. "I'm no chicken," I yelled. Suddenly, I lost my balance. I screamed as I felt myself go. An excited roar came up from down below. Then a strong arm was around my waist, hauling me back.

I fell to my knees on the roof and my stomach heaved. He—the guy, Kurt Doyle—leaned over me, breathing hard. "It's okay," he told me, "you're going to be fine."

If I hadn't been so busy being sick, I would have laughed.

CHAPTER 2

Kurt Doyle lied. He didn't take me "home" to Laysner. By the time I was through being sick and ready to come off the roof, a patrol car with blue lights flashing had pulled into the street and was blocking the way out of the apartment building. A broad-shouldered cop met us on the outer steps and told me that I had to come down to the station.

"Somebody called in, said there was a leaper," he explained to Doyle. Then he looked me over as if I were a stuffed dummy. "What's with him? Strung out on something?"

Doyle's voice was raspier than ever. "Just tired and cold and hungry," he said. "I told him he could come home with me."

People were lined up on both sides of the apartment stairs and in the street, too. Other people were hanging out of their windows, listening. In spite of the early spring cold and the wind, they'd come out to take a good look at someone without the guts to do it.

"Hey, take a good look!" I wanted to shout at them,

but all I could do was wrap my arms around myself, shivering and shaking until I felt my bones scrape against each other.

"We've got to take him down to the station," the cop was telling Doyle. "You want to accompany him?"

"Fourth Precinct?"

The cop nodded, looking a bit surprised.

"Okay, then. I've got my van parked behind the building. I'll meet you there."

"Whatever you say." The cop put a hand in the small of my back. "Let's go," he said to me and marched me down to the prowl car. The crowd stirred and muttered, making comments, but I was glad of the warmth inside the car. The cop's partner gave me a blanket to wrap around myself. It was warm, but the smell of it reminded me of juvenile detention centers and jail cells. I should have jumped, I thought bitterly. I didn't need everything to start up again.

The car began to move through the potholes and bright lights of Washington Street, and the big cop, the one who had talked to Doyle, turned around to me. "What's your name, kid?" he asked. I shrugged. "Uncooperative, huh? Runaway?"

I said nothing. I was watching the people hurrying up and down the sidewalks, buried in warm coats, faces held down out of the wind, hurrying home. I wondered how many of them were glad to be *going* home. The emptiness I'd felt on the roof came again and made my eyes water. I knew what would happen, of course. They'd probably hold me at the station because this late in the day it would be hard to get me into any juvenile detention center. I'd sleep in a cell, covered with a blanket that smelled of disinfectant, and then, in the morning, the DSS—Department of Social Services—people would come down and eyeball me and talk to me and ask why in heck I'd run off from that foster family in Wellham.

The prowl car stopped at a police station, and the cops got out and motioned me out of the back. We walked into the building, and the first thing I saw was Doyle standing there talking to some old-timer behind a desk. Both turned to look at me when we came in, and the old cop motioned me over.

"So you're the kid who tried to act like Superman." Very funny, I thought. "What're you called?" he asked.

"I'm Nobody," I said, and the old cop frowned, little faded brown eyes disappearing behind thick, bushy eyebrows.

"You can that stuff and answer when I talk to you!" he shouted.

Kurt Doyle chuckled. "Don't worry about Sergeant Kraemer. His bark is like a pit bull's, but his heart is as soft as custard cream pie. Or it was when we worked together."

Another surprise. I looked Kurt Doyle over carefully. He was old, too, but though his thick hair was white, his eyes weren't faded out. They were the bluest I'd ever seen. The rest of his face was sharp—sharp nose, thin-lipped mouth, furrows between gray eyebrows. Kurt Doyle didn't look like any cream pie—he looked like a guy you wouldn't want to mess with.

"What's your name?" the sergeant repeated.

"Robert Holland."

Sergeant Kraemer nodded and started writing it down.

"Rob, I'd like to get you something to eat," Kurt Doyle said. "When did you eat last?" I told him. "Okay, then. Your stomach won't tolerate any greasy stuff. Milk and cereal, maybe."

Cereal! Sweetness and crunch, and the cool of sweet fresh milk. I felt sick, nauseated, dizzy. I lurched against the edge of the sergeant's desk, and he told me to sit down. While I was doing that and trying to keep the room from spinning, Doyle left. Sergeant Kraemer sucked on his teeth.

"Best damn cop we had on the force," he said with feeling. "Had to quit when his heart started acting up, see. A sad day, I'm telling you." The faded eyes looked me up and down again. "You a runaway? From where?" I told him. "Didn't it work out?" I shook my head. "Talkative, huh? You got parents? No? *A* parent, maybe?"

"My father . . ." and right away, Pa was near me, his blunt, bullet-shaped head covered by fringes of dark hair, his eyes raking me up and down, big hands hanging by his sides, with the fists flexing as if getting ready to hit at something—me.

Sergeant Kraemer just wrote it all down. "What will you do with me?" I asked.

"What do you care? You were ready to off yourself by jumping tonight." He glanced at me. "How did you get on the roof? Were you going to rob the place, or what?"

"It was cold," I said. "I just pushed some buzzers

outside the door and someone buzzed me in. There were people in the hall, so I just kept walking up the stairs . . ." Kept walking until suddenly, there was the door to the flat roof, kept walking out the door and back into the wind and right up to the edge of the roof.

"You clean?" he was asking me.

"I don't do drugs." He lifted his eyebrows. "I don't drink, either." I thought about how I used to look for Pa, scuttling through alleys at night with my throat thick with fear. I thought of finding him, drunk and sick and smelling of liquor and vomit, and of trying to get him home with him fighting me all the way. And those drunk tanks Pa used to get himself locked into . . . "I don't do those things."

"Fine by me. You're a boy scout. Last time you saw your father?"

"In Boston. We came up from Louisiana because one of Pa's brothers died. Pa used to live in Boston."

"You're a ward of the state, then."

I stiffened my shoulders as the outer door banged open, and Kurt Doyle came through with a sack in his hands. "Eat slow," he said.

I nearly cried when I saw the food. There was a plastic bowl, the kind they sell in supermarkets, and cereal and two cartons of milk. Doyle got me a paper cup from the coffee machine and poured milk for me. It was a good thing. My hands were shaking so much I could hardly hold the plastic spoon he handed me. "Slowly," he commanded. "You eat slow. Chew a hundred times. Didn't your mother ever tell you that?"

"She's dead," I mumbled, and began to eat. The

milk was cool and sweet as it went down. The cereal tasted like something made in heaven. I heard someone making this funny noise and realized that it was me, sobbing as I ate. The two old guys watched me for a minute, then Doyle took the sergeant aside and they talked between themselves.

It took me a while to finish the cereal and then the milk, and by then I was so tired I didn't want to do anything but stretch out and go to sleep. I didn't even care about the cell, as long as there was a blanket in it and a mattress so I could sleep. I looked around for Doyle, found that he was standing behind me.

"You ready to go?" he asked. I blinked at him. There was something wrong with my eyes. The old man seemed to get bigger, then smaller. "Time to go home," the old man went on.

"We were going to keep you here tonight and call the DSS people in the morning, but Kurt says he's taking you home," Sergeant Kraemer said gruffly. "No halfway homes with vacancies and no room at any juvenile detention center, either." He turned to Doyle. "You sure you want to do this? You're responsible for him if we release him to you. Kids like this could be trouble!"

Kurt just smiled and opened the door for me. "I know about trouble," he said, and then he added, "It's a long ride. You can sleep all the way home, son."

But when I got in Kurt Doyle's old, beat-up van, I couldn't sleep. I was tired enough, but as we drove along, questions kept jumping into my head. I could hear the voices of the people who wanted me to jump off the building. "They really did want me to jump," I said finally.

"People like violence," he told me. "Lots of people are hurting and so they want to hurt others." He turned to glance at me, and I felt myself cringe. I hadn't had a good wash for days, and I knew what the old boy must be thinking. Not much to look at, that's what he was thinking—a hunted, timid, rabbity looking wimp of a kid, tall, gawky, with too-thin arms and legs, a too-small face capped with thick dark hair that fell into big, scared brown eyes. And dirty. Hurriedly, I jammed my hands—filthy hands—into my pockets. I'd washed them that morning in a men's room in one of the garages on Tremont Street, but the place was grungy and it stank and I couldn't wash all over like I wanted to. Now, I was crusted with dirt. Pa had always laughed at me for wanting to keep clean. He said it was sissy.

And my jeans—they weren't much better, either. My jeans had holes all the way up my leg, and there was a big patch I'd tried to put in myself near the crotch. There was one big torn flap over my sneakers, and my sneakers were torn, too, so's you could see the dirty toes underneath.

I was ashamed, and I hated Kurt for looking at me. I turned away from him, looked out the van window. Buildings whipped past and street lamps, with halos around the bulbs.

"Your father," Kurt Doyle said into the quiet. "Do you know where he is now?"

I didn't want to talk about Pa, so I shook my head.

"The DSS people took you away from him. That it?"

"Guess so." He was still waiting, so I said, "They took me away because of a child abuse complaint the neighbors made."

The rasp in his voice became harsher. "I'm not trying to be nosy, Rob. You're kind of my responsibility right now, though, and I need to know about you." Pause. "He drink?"

I nodded, feeling cornered in the van with Doyle. I didn't know anything about him, just that he was an ex-cop with a heart problem. Maybe he read my mind, because he sort of cleared his throat.

"Fair's fair," he rumbled. "I'm a widower, Rob, and I live by myself. My wife and I had one daughter . . . she lives in California." He ran a hand through his white hair before adding, "I'm fifty-eight years old, and I retired from the force because of heart trouble. I work in Laysner, as a warehouse guard. I work some days, some nights, and I have a fondness for boats."

That meant I now knew about him? I saw from the sharp set of his profile that he was frowning. Well, he was probably realizing what he'd let himself in for! "I ran away from my last foster home," I said.

"Are you warning me?" Amusement? I couldn't tell. "Were they too strict for you?" I shrugged. "Or didn't you fit in?"

He was sharp, this guy. Being a cop all those years would teach you a few things. No, I hadn't fit in. I hadn't belonged. But that hadn't surprised me. It had just made me leave.

"I'll try not to lay too many rules on you, Rob," Doyle was saying. "I'll only ask that we be honest with each other. All right?" I mumbled an okay. "Do you want to talk about your father?" he continued.

No, I thought, I do not. But my mind slid back through the months, the years. "Mostly we followed crops," I said. "We'd start in Texas and work our way up to Colorado for the watermelon season. Other times, Pa found work on the docks. He's real strong, not like me."

"You look pretty healthy to me."

"You know what I mean. Pa could lift a hundred pounds in one hand. He's a big guy." I couldn't believe what I was doing—I was bragging about Pa! "One time in Louisiana, this big fisherman picked on him, and Pa just threw the guy into the water. Threw him right in."

I glanced at Doyle to see how he was taking this, but he just kept on driving. The frown still creased his brows. "You had some good times together, then."

"Yeah, sometimes." But the lie caught in my throat.

"And sometimes he drank, and then he hit you," Doyle continued.

More than sometimes, but I didn't say anything because, really, it hadn't been the beatings I'd minded most. They hurt, but bruises went away and bones mended. It was the words. Pa could lash out at me, and the words would hurt so much that I'd want to do anything to escape them. *Stupid, useless, rotten creep*—all those words that had been used instead of my name.

"I gather he abused you for some time," Doyle said dryly. "When did the DSS people do something about it?"

I didn't want to think about that time, either, but I told him. "When we were in Boston. We'd come up for

Uncle Ted's funeral and stayed a few months. Pa was almost out of money and went drinking. I was worried because there wasn't any food in the house."

Worried? I'd been sick. I'd tried to find Pa but couldn't. And then he'd come home and blamed me for there being no money left. He blamed me, and then he beat me.

"He hit me bad. I guess he went out of control," I explained to Doyle. "The neighbors called the police and they took me to the hospital." The 51-A—the beatings—had resulted in my being made a ward of the state. "There was Family Court, the whole bit. Pa signed statements handing me over."

Creep. Yellowbelly. Idiot. Why-don't-you-die? It's your fault that I'm trapped. Stinking little jerk.

And all the times he'd said those things to me, I'd been waiting. Just waiting to hear him say one kind, one good or loving thing. If Pa had hugged me once, I wouldn't have cared how many bones he broke. I'd have said see-you-later to the courts and taken after him. Had Pa ever hugged me? Ever? He must have . . .

I knew I was fading out of reality. The aching tiredness had caught up with me. My head was nodding back and forth, snapping me awake and then letting me fall back to sleep. The warmth and the hum of the van were getting the better of me, taking me over.

"Here," Doyle said. He unbuttoned his overcoat, took it off, and threw it over me. "Wrap up and get some sleep. It's going to be a long ride."

"Just for a little," I mumbled. I wasn't going to fall asleep if I could help it. How did I know this tough ex-cop was really taking me to Laysner? I didn't trust him all that much.

And yet, in spite of everything, my eyes closed, and I was gone.

CHAPTER 3

I dreamed that I was five years old again and that it was my first day at Cramston Elementary, down in Texas. Mom was sick then, so sick that she couldn't get up to help me dress for my first day of school, and I'd forgotten to put on my socks. In my dream I tried to act friendly, even though I was scared when all the kids came up to me and stood around in a kind of circle, watching me.

Then, a big kid pushed through the circle and started to look me over. He started to snicker, and he pointed to my feet. The other kids nudged each other and giggled and pointed, too, and then they all shouted, "He doesn't have any socks on his feet! This boy doesn't have what it takes! He's chicken and he's stupid and he'll never make it. Why don't you jump, Rob Holland? Why don't you jump . . . jump . . . *jump?*"

I came awake twitching and jerking and making sobbing noises in my throat. I didn't know where I was for a minute, and then I heard the sounds of the van.

"We're almost there," Doyle said in his deep, raspy voice. "You've slept most of the way."

I sat up and looked out the van window. It was dark, but I could see we were traveling down a long, winding country road. I could see the white fronts of houses and the tall shade trees clustered around the fences. I turned from the window, rubbed the back of my neck. It felt stiff; I felt stiff. If anything, I felt more tired than I'd been before falling asleep.

"Here we are, Peach Street," Kurt Doyle was saying in a satisfied voice. He slowed the van and turned a corner, then coasted down easy for a few yards. "Not much," he said, "but home is home."

We'd stopped in front of a house that was small enough to be called a cottage. A streetlight, shining down on the pickup and the front yard of the house, made it seem very bright against the darkness. Kurt got out and nodded for me to follow.

It was cold outside. There was a tang in the air, the smell of the sea carried on the night wind. I stretched to unbend the kinks of the long ride and followed Doyle up a pebbled walkway to the little house and up onto the porch. A couple of wooden chairs stood on the porch, and there was a big metal dog dish near the door. At the same moment, a loud barking began.

"You've got a dog?" I asked.

He grinned. "He likes to think so," he said. Then he opened the front door and out waddled a small, black cocker spaniel. He was the fattest thing I'd ever seen. "This is Elmer," Doyle said. "He's about 105 on the human scale, but he has yet to behave like a senior citizen." The dog was wrinkling his nose at me. "Let him sniff you all over. He doesn't see so well any more."

Elmer commenced sniffing me in an interested way. His large, wet nose went everywhere. I didn't mind. People look at your sideways and sneak glances when you're not looking, give you the once-over without ever being up-front about it. Elmer's curiosity was honest. When he'd finished, he decided I was okay and gave my hand a lick. I rubbed behind his ears and he began to wag his stub of a tail.

"You've passed inspection," Doyle said dryly. "Elmer, get out of our way and let us in."

Old Elmer wagged himself through the door, leading us into the house. Doyle switched on a light that shone over a small, dark-paneled room with a messy fireplace, and even messier tables with clusters of photos and magazines and newspapers all over them. There was also an easy chair and a couch covered with old blankets.

"This is it," Doyle said. "Suit you?"

I nodded. It wasn't a bad place, but it sure was messy. I thought of the house in Wellham where my ex-foster mother had chased every spot and dust speck with a broom and a mop. She'd never have lasted here!

Doyle was watching me out of those sharp blue eyes. "I'm not much of a housekeeper," he said, not apologizing but telling it like it was. "Still, it's better than some police jail cell. Come on, now, and I'll show you where you can sleep." He paused, adding offhandedly, "And maybe you'd like to take a shower. I could find some clothes for you. You're taller than me, but what I have will do for now."

He led the way through a hall that divided into a kitchen on one side and a couple of bedrooms on the other. Doyle led me into the smaller bedroom.

"Used to be my girl's," he said, abruptly. I looked around. The room had a cot in it, a small chest of drawers, a desk, a round bedside table. There was a braided rug on the floor and curtains in the windows. It was a nice room, but there was a lot of dust around.

"It's fine," I said. Doyle was looking at me. He was, I figured, probably asking himself why he'd brought me here to his house.

"Glad you think so. Across from you is the shower. There are towels and there's soap in there already, and I'll get you stuff to wear."

I stayed in the shower for almost an hour. It'd been such a long time since I'd felt soap and hot water, and I scrubbed my skin till it hurt. I stood under the gush of the hot water and lathered myself again and again, until there was hardly anything left of the bar of soap.

Pa had hated washing. The only time he tried to clean himself up was before he went looking for one of his occasional jobs. Whenever I took a bath, Pa would look at me like I was crazy. "Washing yourself won't wash your stink away," he'd say.

I washed myself harder, remembering, and rubbed my fingers into the scalp under my hair. My hair had grown so long. When they'd got hold of me, the DSS people had cut my hair real short, so it fit my small head like a cap. They'd found clean clothes for me, a nearly new shirt, tie, clean pants. Even new sneakers! Pa had stared at me that day when we met before the Family Court judge. And then he'd said it.

I didn't want to remember what Pa had said. I shut off the hot shower and stood in the steam, trying not to remember. But Pa's voice came anyway, like it always did. "I tried and tried to help this boy. He's an animal. Don't know right from wrong . . ."

"No," I whispered, but the remembered words kept coming.

"He's got a face like his mother's . . . an angel's, but he's got a mean, dishonest streak in him . . ."

Pa, I thought, no. I won't remember!

". . . I never want to see him again, your Honor. You people want him? Take him with my blessing!"

I squeezed my eyes shut and bit my lower lip so hard I tasted blood. I hadn't cried in the courtroom when Pa said that, but I cried now. I stood in the hot, steamy shower like a fool, with tears running down my cheeks.

"Hey . . . you okay in there, boy?" Doyle shouted.

I realized that I was shaking, and the water was starting to run cold. "I'm fine!" I called. I knew I'd better hurry. I didn't want Doyle to get mad at me. I dried myself quickly and then found folded clothes by the door. The dungarees were too short and too big around the waist, and the flannel shirt was too short in the arms and too big in the shoulders, but Doyle had left me my own belt. It went through the loops of the jeans like an old friend.

I spent a few more minutes inside the bathroom,

cleaning up after myself. I hung up the towels that Doyle had thrown all over the floor, wiped out the stall and the washbasin. I was just finishing when Doyle knocked on the bathroom door. He lifted his eyebrows when he saw what I was doing, but all he said was, "You about ready to eat?"

A delicious smell was coming from the kitchen, and my stomach started to gurgle. I smelled hot chocolate and, with it, bacon, pancakes, syrup. I followed Doyle down the hallway to the small kitchen. There was a table covered with a red vinyl cloth, and on it was a plate of eggs, pancakes, bacon. Two mugs were on the table but only one heaped plate and only one knife and fork.

Doyle waved me to the plate. "Dig in," he invited in his rusty voice.

I didn't need to be asked twice. I shoveled the food into my mouth as fast as it would go, washing it down with the hot chocolate. Doyle said nothing, just sipped from his mug and waited. Elmer came to sit beside me and pushed his nose onto my lap.

"Can I give him something?" I asked, mouth full.

"Why not? Elmer has it in his mind that he's human. If you gave him a knife and fork, he'd eat like a person," Doyle said.

There was no criticism in his voice, none at all, but I looked at my plate and reddened. My hands felt clumsy and rough as I put down the knife and fork and wished I'd taken my time eating. That was dumb. He must think I ate like an animal in the zoo.

"There's more," Doyle offered.

I could have easily eaten another plateful, but I didn't dare. "No, thanks."

"Then, we'll talk." Doyle got up to fill both our mugs with more hot chocolate. "I've been sitting in the kitchen, Rob, listening to you splash around in the shower. I've been thinking it's some kind of Providence that sent me in to shop downtown Boston tonight of all nights. You know what Providence is?" I shook my head, feeling dumb. He said, "Fate, if you like." Then, he smiled. "Or, the hand of God."

Pa would have thrown back his head and laughed, but I didn't laugh. I just shrugged.

"Well, whatever," Kurt Doyle said easily. "I made you a promise up on the rooftop. It's not a promise I thought to make, mind you. If I'd had the time to think about it, I probably wouldn't have made it. I'm getting on. I've been alone a long time, and I don't enjoy the idea of being responsible for another human being. But I made a promise, and a promise is a promise." He frowned, rubbing his thick, strong hand against his jaw. "I made a call to someone I know while you were in the shower. Rosemary Towers is with the DSS people. She said she'd come by first thing in the morning."

The DSS people. So he *was* getting rid of me.

"Massachusetts allows single people to become foster parents. Rosemary will come in and look us over and make sure it's okay to leave you here with me. The question is, how do you feel about it?"

Not knowing what to make of the question, I shrugged.

"Don't do that," he said irritably. "Do you want to

stay here? Do you have any other place to go, someplace you haven't mentioned? You said you had an uncle in Boston. Maybe you have other kin."

I lowered my eyes and saw Elmer's upturned snout. I rubbed it. "No."

"Then," Doyle said, "you might as well stay here as anywhere else." He spoke in a not very welcoming voice, but he didn't seem mad, either.

"I guess."

There was a longish silence, so I looked up and saw him watching me. "There's extra room here and you're welcome to it," he finally said. "If you stay here, I'll do my best for you. The only thing, as I said before, is for us to stay honest with each other. You have any questions?"

I had plenty, the main one being, why? Why bother if he didn't want me? Nobody cared about breaking promises any more. So if he told a few lies to keep a kid from jumping off a roof, so what?

I said, "No questions."

"Let's wash up and get to bed. Rosemary will be here early." He paused. "I'll be on night shift at the warehouse tomorrow. I have two nights on, three days, then two days off. Rosemary will want to know if you can handle yourself okay while I'm at work."

"I can take care of myself," I said.

It came out sharper than I'd meant, and I looked up at him quick enough to see the scowl form between his eyebrows. Then he grinned wryly. "I'll bet," he said.

I helped him clean up. That is, I did most of the scrubbing and cleaning and mopping while he did the dishes. The place really hadn't been cleaned in a long time, and it was hard to scrape grease off the countertops and stained floor. When I finished, I saw Doyle watching me.

"Best hit the sack," he told me. "I put my pj's on your bed, but they might not fit."

I mumbled my thanks and started to leave the kitchen. As I did so, Pa's voice sneered in my ear. *Why, boy? Why is he doing this? Nobody does a favor without he wants something back. What's in this for Doyle?"*

"Robby," Doyle rasped.

My shoulders tensed. I turned, saw him still watching me. My throat felt dry. "What?" I managed.

He smiled. He sighed. "Sleep well," he said.

In spite of that long sleep in the car, I went out like a light. I slept like a pile of soggy flapjacks, my body sinking miles deep into the soft mattress. I don't know if I dreamed or what I dreamed about, but by the time I opened my eyes, it was morning, and there was a thick slice of sunlight pushing its way through the opening between the window curtains. I lay on the cot for just a minute, then heard the sound of voices in the kitchen.

The DSS lady! Heart banging, I sat up in bed. I'd overslept—they'd be mad at me for that. I jumped out of bed, nearly lost my too-big pajama bottoms, dressed quickly. I only stopped in the bathroom to splash water on my face, comb my hair. Brown eyes stared back at me uncertainly. What were they saying about me in the kitchen?

The Department of Social Services people could do anything they wanted with me. They'd done that before. After Pa, there'd been two foster homes. I went down the hall quickly and heard Doyle say: "The question is whether or not you'll let me keep him here, Rosemary."

"I'm wondering why you'd want to," a woman's voice replied. I stopped where I was, listening. "You've been living alone for many years, Kurt. You're set in your ways. And you and Alma didn't get on all that well."

There was a little silence. Then, "Alma has nothing to do with this," Doyle said. He sounded grim.

"I think we need to talk about your daughter, Kurt. I know it's a painful subject, but you and Alma had some rocky times. You didn't see eye to eye on many things. Are you ready to take on another teenager, one you know nothing about?"

Doyle's voice was even more grim. "I made a promise."

"A promise made to stop a suicide doesn't bind you."

Doyle cleared his throat. "I may have acted instinctively, but a promise is a promise. I feel responsible for the boy."

"He'll upset your life-style," the DSS lady warned. "Rob Holland has more than his share of problems. The file on him shows abuse by the father . . ."

I figured that it was time to walk into the kitchen. There was a slim, elderly woman sitting near Doyle at the kitchen table.

"This is Mrs. Towers," Doyle said, and the social

worker lady smiled at me. She had a neat, efficient smile, and her eyes looked me over quickly. When Doyle got up to pour coffee, she nodded to me to come sit beside her.

"I need to ask you some questions, Rob. Looking at your file, I see that you didn't go to school very much."

"I went off and on," I said. Doyle put a mug of coffee in front of me and I made this big thing of sipping and stirring, so I wouldn't have to meet Mrs. Towers's probing eyes. "I went to school in Texas, while Mom was alive. Then in Louisiana some, while Pa was working the fishing boats there. Afterwards, there were a few weeks here, a few weeks there."

"You mean, between crops," Doyle said. I nodded. It wasn't legal, but nobody cared much about the law come harvest time. Pa always figured four hands could pick better than two.

Mrs. Towers pushed a pencil and a pad of paper over to me. "Rob, I'd like you to do something for me. Write a few sentences down. About anything." I guess my face looked blank. "I need to see how well you can write," she explained.

I knew that this was where I'd prove how dumb I was. I glanced at Doyle, but his sharp mouth was stern, and he nodded. Do it.

Write, she'd said. About what? I frowned, moving the pencil around between my fingers. "*Can* you write, Rob?" Mrs. Towers asked then, really gently. I felt my face get hot, and I nodded and wrote out a few sentences, real fast. I shoved the pad over to Mrs. Towers, who frowned as she took it, and then frowned some more. "Who taught you to write, Rob?" I shrugged and told her, my mother. Mom had read stories to me, and she'd got me started reading and writing even though I was little when she died. I hoped Mrs. Tower wouldn't ask me any more questions. The memory of my mother was dim and blurry, but thinking about her hurt.

Mrs. Tower asked me other questions. How long had I lived in Louisiana? Where had we lived? Did I have any good friends? She wrote down all the answers I gave, then smiled at Doyle.

"I think it'll be all right, Kurt. I'll make a favorable report of my home-study visit."

I glanced questioningly at Doyle, who said, "That means we're stuck with each other."

"The father has already signed papers saying he agrees to let the state take custody. I feel that you'll be given temporary approval pending completion of paperwork. Naturally you'll have to attend parent training classes, Kurt." He grunted. "You'll be going to Laysner Secondary School, Rob."

Doyle explained that this was a seventh through twelfth grade school. I didn't like what he was saying. Maybe I could read some and write, but compared to kids my age, I was so far back it wasn't funny.

While I was thinking this, Doyle walked Mrs. Towers to the door. Elmer followed them, so I was left alone in the sunny kitchen. There was a tightness in my chest, but I told myself to quit worrying. Whatever happened to me, nothing could possibly be as bad as what had happened before. Even if Doyle wanted to wash his hands of me, I'd been left on my own before.

Yesterday, I'd been ready to take a quick walk off a roof to finish all my problems. And, though right now my stomach was full and the kitchen was warm and bright, nothing really had changed.

If things didn't work out for me here, there'd always be another rooftop someplace else.

CHAPTER 4

Doyle took me into town and bought me some clothes at a dinky little clothing store. He bought me two pairs of dungarees, work boots, two flannel shirts, underwear, and a pair of blue-and-white sneakers.

"Don't worry about it," he told me. "The DSS people give me money for your upkeep."

Then we went grocery shopping. "Elmer and me, we don't eat too much," Doyle explained. "You're different. Growing kids have to eat."

Eat wasn't the word. In the next few days, while we waited for Mrs. Towers to do her thing and get me "placed" with Doyle, I really pigged out. I didn't mean to, and every time we sat down at the table I'd tell myself, Robby, for crying out loud, don't stuff your face. I would remember how Pa, one time, emptied my plate onto the floor and told me to eat on the ground because I bolted my food like a pig. "You ain't fit to eat with a human," he'd said. So I tried to eat less when Doyle put food on the table, but I'd crave the food so much I couldn't help it.

"For Pete's sake, will you please eat?" Doyle would finally say. "You're as skinny as a pipestem. No need to hold back."

I tried to make up for eating so much by doing stuff around the house. At first, that nearly caused a blowout. Doyle came in from work one time and found me on my hands and knees scrubbing the grease off the kitchen floor. He stood there in his gray guard's uniform, thick fingers hooked into his belt, frowning like there was no tomorrow.

"Leave that," he said. I looked up at him. "I know you like things neat. Better get one thing straight, though. I am a slob and will continue to be one. Twenty years of marriage didn't change me, and neither will you."

I sensed the warning—don't think you can change any part of me or the way I live. I felt like I'd done something shameful, and I didn't know whether to try to explain or just do as he said.

"Leave it!" He was really riled now.

I blurted it out. "It's nothing to do with you. After Mom died, Pa and I lived in filth. So's I could stand it, I had to try to clean—it's a habit."

I was shaking as the words trailed off, and Elmer whined and shoved his cold nose against my cheek, whuffing gently.

"Leave it," Doyle said in a quieter voice. "It's too nice a day to be on your hands and knees scrubbing a floor." But he wasn't mad any more, and later he didn't complain when I started to straighten up the rest of his house, throwing out papers three years old and bottles and stacks of magazines. He even pitched in when I got to the garage, and, while I was working to get the stains off the concrete floor, he showed me his tools and what they were used for.

There was a lot of boat stuff in the garage, too. "One of these days we're going for a spin on the *Dragonfly,*" he promised me. "Maybe when my days off come around."

Doyle was at work, and I was carrying out trash from the garage when Mrs. Towers came by a few days later. She blinked in surprise. "He's got you working, I see," she remarked. I said that I didn't mind, and she asked where Doyle was. "I stopped by to tell you both the news—Kurt's been awarded temporary custody." She paused. "Have you been registered at school yet?"

I mumbled that we hadn't gotten around to it. She gave me a look that made me nervous, but all she did was switch the subject. "Has Kurt ever mentioned his daughter, Alma, to you?"

"Once or twice."

"He doesn't like to talk about her." Mrs. Towers chewed her bottom lip as if turning something over in her mind. "Since you and Kurt will be living together, I think I should explain to you that Alma ran away from home."

"No way," I exclaimed. I was really surprised. Quickly she added that it hadn't been Kurt's fault.

"He loved Alma. She was his only child. But he was also very strict, especially after his wife passed away." Mrs. Towers hesitated. "You see, in those days he was a policeman, and I suppose what he saw in his line of work made him want to keep Alma safe. She thought that he didn't trust her. They fought. Eventually she ran away from home and went to live with an aunt in California."

I asked what had happened to Alma, and Mrs. Towers said that she'd stayed with her aunt, gone to school, and married there. "Kurt didn't go to the wedding. He's very bitter about it, angry at the whole world. That's why I was surprised when he took you in."

I was glad Mrs. Towers had leveled with me. It explained why Doyle sometimes looked at me with that bitter look in his sharp blue eyes. Then I quit worrying about Doyle and started thinking about myself. The thought of going to school was like having a cage measured for me.

Doyle himself drove me to Laysner Secondary next morning. "What are you doing? he asked me as I carefully checked my socks before we left the house. I shrugged, and he looked me up and down. "You look really duded up," he told me. "You nervous?"

I was shaking so hard that my ribs were scraping together. My hands were sweating, and I couldn't feel my toes. As we drove down Peach Street, I tried to concentrate on what Doyle was saying, but all I could remember was other schools, other first days. I swallowed hard, but I couldn't rid myself of the bitter taste of my own fear.

It was a pretty, early spring day. In the morning sunlight Laysner looked like any of the small towns that Pa and I had traveled through. The streets were lined with saltbox houses, small front yards ready for spring green, soil turned for backyard vegetables. On Main, the central artery of the town, there were a few stores, a hardware shop, post office, library, and a combined police-fire department. A little way off, a tall church pointed its spire into the blue sky.

We turned off Main and swung onto a long road that wound beside a seawall. Doyle jerked over his shoulder with his thumb. "The warehouse where I work is that way. I'll take you there one of these days. Up ahead is the school. You can see it now."

I didn't want to look, but of course I did. It looked about as I'd expected, a big, flat-topped cinder block building surrounded by trees. There was an athletics field at one end, tennis courts on the other. I remembered how one time I'd tried to get on some kind of team—baseball, I think—and Pa had laughed at me so hard for wanting to try that I'd never shown up to even one game.

"Here we are," Doyle said.

It was past eight, and the steps and the corridor of the school were empty. I followed Doyle into the office. There was a middle-aged secretary and, sitting on a wooden bench by the door, there were two guys. One was dark-haired and chunky, the other had red hair and freckles and water-pale blue eyes. They gave me the once-over as I stood behind Doyle.

"Hey, Dan," Redhead whispered loudly. "Another ree-cruit for the Dummy Room."

They both snickered, and the other kid's fat black eyes went over me with contempt. I turned my back on them. The secretary gave me a quick little smile and told Doyle and me to come with her, please.

She marched us into the principal's office, and a short, harassed individual shook my hand with a damp claw and welcomed me to tne school. Then he called in a Mrs. Sidman, the head of the guidance department, who asked us to step into her office.

She had a file on me, and while she talked she kept looking at it. "Rob, you . . . ah . . . haven't had much consistent education. There are no records or tests to speak of, so we'd like to core you. That means test you and see what classes you'd most likely fit into."

I knew where I fit into. That redhead had me pegged. The Dummy Room, wherever that was. Doyle gave me a dig in the ribs. "Tests won't hurt you," he growled. Much he knew!

Mrs. Sidman took over. She told Doyle he could go home, that I'd make it back on the school bus. Then, with Doyle gone, she took me down a silent corridor to a room marked RC32. She swung the door open, and I stepped into a big room scattered with chairs and round tables. Kids were either working in groups, or just shooting the bull and laughing. One kid was doing a Beastie Boys imitation.

"Hey, Mr. Fitz," someone said, "here's some new kid."

A big guy who'd been sitting with a bunch of kids got up and came toward us. He looked tired, but he smiled when Mrs. Sidman introduced us. "Rob," he said, and shook my hand. "We'll get to that testing right away.

Sit down and sort of get used to the surroundings, okay?"

I took a corner chair and watched Mrs. Sidman leave and Mr. Fitz work with his group. The guy who'd been doing imitations now sat down and started to make foghorn noises. I wanted to get the heck out of there, but I didn't move. They were all watching me while pretending not to, and I knew a lot of that foghorn junk was for my benefit. After a while, one of the other kids came over and asked me if I was really new in town.

"No fooling?" he asked and then added, "It's a crummy town." He had pale hair and serious brown eyes and a nervous way of blinking. "There's no action here. None. Where are you from?" I said, all over. "Well, you'll be bored out of your skull in this town," he went on. "It's the pits. School is a jail, especially in here. Do you know what it's called?"

"RC32," I said, and he snorted and blinked.

"We're called the Dummy Room," he said. "We aren't all dumb," he added, explaining, "but that's what they call us anyway."

I glanced over to where Mr. Fitz was telling Foghorn to cool it. "That's enough for today, Jerry," he said.

"You gonna get cored?" the pale kid wanted to know. "I got cored once. Man, they test you out of your skull and you get to look at stupid little inkblots and then the shrink asks you dumb questions."

He looked at me for my reaction, but, before I could say anything, the period buzzer went off, scaring me to death. Everybody scrambled for the door, and

Foghorn started up loud and clear as he left the room. Mr. Fitz mumbled something under his breath, then turned to me and smiled.

"Good," he said. "You survived. Well, now, you and I are going to have some time together. You ever been tested or cored before, Rob? Of course, you won't be expected to finish all these today . . ."

It was pretty much like what the twitchy kid had said. There were tests. Most of them were pretty easy. I had to look at circles, then at pictures, then at words that matched or didn't, triangles, squares, numbers. Before I was through, the period buzzer went again, and a new crop of kids came into the room. These kids were quieter, though, and soon got to work in a friendly, easy way that made me envy them.

After I'd finished the tests, Mrs. Sidman came by again and took me to see somebody called Dr. Braun, the shrink, who made me look at the inkblots and draw pictures. He wrote down what I said and did and asked me questions about my life with Pa, school, how I felt about myself. He finally got to the nitty-gritty: Why had I tried to jump off a rooftop? I said I was tired and hungry, which was mostly true, anyway. He put down his pen and looked at me, hard.

"Are you angry at your father, Robert?" he asked.

Angry at Pa? I sucked in a deep breath and thought about that. I guess I'd been angry plenty of times, but what I remembered most was the fear.

From the shrink I went to lunch. Mrs. Sidman took me there but from then on I was on my own. I stood in that loud, crowded cafeteria looking around for the pale, twitchy kid, or even Foghorn, anyone who looked familiar, but there was no one, just a mass of screaming kids lining up for school food. When I got a tray there wasn't any place to sit down, because everyone seemed to be sitting with their friends. I wished myself a hundred miles away. I wished I could crawl into some corner and hide. I had the biggest urge to check and see if I had my socks on . . .

"It really is yucky food, isn't it?"

I looked, surprised, wondering if someone had spoken to me, and saw a girl beside me. She was looking for a seat, too, and she gave me a smile. "You new?" she asked.

I nodded. She had a heart-shaped face and a spill of dark hair, a sprinkle of freckles across the bridge of a snub nose. "Debbie!" somebody shouted. "Debbie Carmody!"

She gave me a smile again and went off to join her friends, her dark hair swinging. A few steps away from me, she paused, turning her head over her shoulder. "Come on," she told me. "There's room down at that table."

But before I could move, Mrs. Sidman was beside me again. "Rob, you through with lunch?"

I said I was. I didn't want to eat, anyway. Besides, I never would have had the guts to join Debbie Carmody at that table. I thought of her, though, as I finished the last test of the afternoon, then sat in RC32 watching Mr. Fitz teach. I wondered if he was going to be my teacher. I wouldn't have minded.

The classroom door swung open and two kids

sauntered in. They were the two I'd seen in the office that morning. "Hey, Fitz," Redhead said, "we're late."

I saw Mr. Fitz's face change. He looked hard and angry. "You've got a pass, Seth? Dan?"

The two began to nudge each other. "We got a pass, Dan?" Seth, the redhead, asked.

"Sure . . . someplace!" The fat kid patted his pockets, faked a look of misery. "Somebody ripped us off, Fitz. Somebody picked my pocket."

Mr. Fitz sighed. "You know the rules. Down to the office and get a pass."

Everybody was looking at those two, which was what they wanted. "No way we're going to that office again," Seth said. He looked around the room. His eyes lit on me, and he grinned. "Hey, Fitzie, it's cool. We'll just sit here quiet-like and help the new kid. We'll tell him about this great school, Fitz."

I could see Mr. Fitz trying to decide. He was tired, so he shrugged. "Okay, just be quiet," he sighed.

I watched Dan wink at Seth as they closed in on me. My hands felt clammy. They sat down, one on each side of me. "Hey, new kid," Seth began, "you like the Dummy Room?"

I shrugged. I was shaking, and I hated myself for it. Why did I start shaking whenever I got nervous? I twisted my sweating hands into my pockets. If these two picked on me, I'd get up and walk out that door. I would . . .

"Cut it out, Seth," Dan said. "He's new. He's probably an okay kid. Say, where you from, anyway?" I said, all over. "What does your old man do?"

I hesitated. "He's not here. I'm living with a . . . friend."

"Lucky," Seth grunted. "What I wouldn't give to be away from *my* old man!" They looked at me with a new envy, and Seth dipped into his pants pocket. "Hey, you want one?"

I reached automatically before I saw what it was—the small nub of a joint. "Keep it down," Dan warned. "Don't let Fitz spot you. Didn't you never see a bone before?"

Just then, the RC32 door swung open, and Debbie Carmody walked in. She was carrying an armful of books and her dark hair swung behind her, catching the light. "Hi, Mr. Fitz," she said.

"Hello, Debbie." A real smile crossed the teacher's tired face. "You're late today."

"I had to make up a quiz," she said. I stared. She was in *this* room? She saw me stare, turned to smile at me, then saw Dan and Seth. The smile dried up and she swung away, turning her back on us. Seth winked at me and whistled.

"Stop that!" Mr. Fitz roared. "One more noise and you're out of here, Seth Boudine!"

Seth fell to his knees. "Oh, sir! Oh, Mr. Fitz, *suh!* Don't send me away!"

Mr. Fitz's face was as red as a brick. "You get out!" He bellowed. He pulled a pink pass out of his shirt pocket, scribbled on it madly. "Get out of here!"

"Hey, I'm going, man," Seth said. He took the pink pass, waved it at Dan and me. "See you guys around!"

Dan waved both his arms, but I didn't know what

to do. Mr. Fitz was staring at me. "Rob, come over here," he said, sternly.

I got up and walked, stiff-legged, to where Mr. Fitz and Debbie were standing. Mr. Fitz said, "You're new here, so I want to clue you in. We have rules." He glared at the grinning Dan. "I wouldn't want you to start out on the wrong foot, get in with the wrong crowd."

Debbie was watching me, not saying anything, just watching. "Do you understand what I'm saying?" Mr. Fitz demanded.

I nodded.

"Mrs. Sidman will probably assign you to a few periods a day in RC32. We'll help you here. But you have to help yourself, too." He looked at me, at Dan, then back at me.

I pulled my hands out of my pockets and started to tell him, yes, I understood, but instead my heart dropped onto the floor. The joint that Seth had passed to me fell out of my pants pocket! In horror, I saw it on the ground next to my foot. I moved my sneaker quick to cover it, but not quick enough. Both Debbie and Mr. Fitz saw it. Debbie gave me a disgusted look and turned her back. Dan began to laugh.

"Pick that filthy thing up and throw it away!" Mr. Fitz hissed. He sounded really mad, but the look on his face was worse. He looked sad and disgusted.

I wanted to cry, to explain, to get out of there! Instead, I bent down and picked up the joint and started toward the trash.

"Not in my classroom!" Mr. Fitz snapped.

The buzzer went. Dan's laughter exploded through the room. "Oh, man alive, oh, Ro-bee, we want you to start out on the right foot! Bus-ted!" Whooping, he ran from the room.

CHAPTER 5

Doyle asked me how school had gone. I said, okay. He asked me how the tests were. "Hated tests when I was your age," he told me. "Used to go into a class knowing every dang thing, but when I looked at those tests, everything in my brain would wither away. I always did badly on tests."

I didn't know what to say, so I shrugged. I saw the flicker of irritation in his eyes, but I couldn't help it. What could I say—I loused up my first day at school, and now the teacher thinks I'm a jerk? To say nothing about Debbie.

"You meet anyone?" Doyle continued.

I thought of Seth and Dan. "Not yet. I didn't have much time," I lied.

"You will. Once you get some friends, it won't be so bad." He was being nice, I knew, but I wished he'd just leave me alone. I wanted to be by myself. The thought of school made my insides feel raw. But Doyle wasn't about to leave me be. "There's some daylight left," he said. "We can take the *Dragonfly* for a sail. It's not that cold out."

I shrugged. I didn't want to go, but I didn't have the guts to say so. I figured Doyle's boat was his pride and joy, and if I said I didn't feel like a sail, he'd give up on me completely.

He made me help him get ready, carry the tiller and sail and extra lifejacket to the van and load them in. We drove down Peach and onto Main and up the winding road that took us to the sea. There was a parking area near the seawall. We got out of the van and the tangy, salt smell of the sea made me remember Louisiana, but this was different. There, salt and fish came to you on gusts of moist warm air. Here, everything was raw and angry. I shivered.

"Wrap this extra jacket around you," Doyle said, "and then carry this on down those steps over there. They lead to what we Laysner sailors call our marina. Nothing fancy, really, but the *Dragonfly* is happy there."

He spoke of the boat as if it was a real person, and what's more, a person he liked. He smiled as he talked about the *Dragonfly,* but the scowl came back real quick when he saw a group of guys leaning up against the seawall, watching the waves and pitching pebbles into the water. He glared at them and grunted, sort of, under his breath, something about riffraff. Then, he nodded to me to walk down the steps and out to the marina.

"Hey, Officer Doyle!"

Doyle's frown deepened, but he turned his head to look at the big, dark-bearded guy who'd called out to him. He didn't say anything, just looked. I looked, too. The big guy wore an expensive-looking jacket and designer jeans, and he had dark hair and bold gray eyes and a scraggly beard that started near his ears and wound all over his chin. He was smiling.

"Nice to see you, Officer. Out for a sail, are you? No business today—just pleasure?"

"No business," Doyle said, snapping off each word and using a voice I'd never heard before. "Get lost, Jason."

Jason, the big guy, and the others with him just sort of grinned and watched Doyle, whose face was getting red, the veins standing out against his neck. "Just thought I'd ask, Officer," Jason said, softly. I thought Doyle was going to start screaming and hollering, he looked so mad! Instead, he turned and headed for the long, slender quay where the boats were. He pointed to a white boat with a red stripe around it.

"There she is, Rob," he said. I could hear him still struggling with his anger. "Prettiest boat that ever sailed."

She *was* pretty, for sure. She sat saucily on the water, dipping back and forth. Doyle led the way down the quay then turned to me again. "She's close enough on the dock so we won't need to paddle out to her. But watch me. Don't fall in," he warned.

He went aboard the boat with surprising swiftness, took the stuff from my arms, and stowed it. He helped me onto the *Dragonfly.* I watched as he let down the centerboard, attached the rudder and tiller, unmoored the boat.

"You been in a boat before?" he asked me.

"One time. Pa was working the fishing boats down in Louisiana, and they needed help bad." I didn't tell Doyle the rest, that I'd gotten sick on the stormy sea with the stink of shrimp and fish and nets. And had Pa whaled me for that one!

"This isn't a fishing trawler," Doyle said. "Watch, now. We're lying head-to-wind, so we can hoist the sails. Mainsail goes on first, jib next."

I watched his hands, square and strong and chunky, move gracefully about the work. But when the mainsail was hoisted, it looked wrinkled. Doyle saw me looking, smiled a bit. "The wrinkles will disappear when the wind comes and puffs the sails," he said. "Jib has to be loose, too. Otherwise—" he paused. "Well, looky there."

He was pointing at another boat on the water, some distance from us. This one had a bright orange sail. As I squinted against the late sunlight to see it better, I also saw a line of dark rocks, set like bad teeth, beyond. The rocks seemed to extend in a long, circular line, but through an opening white water showed.

"What's that?" I asked, meaning the rocks. Doyle thought I meant the boat.

"Aaron Carmody," he told me. "The worst sailor in the whole world." As he spoke, a breath of wind puffed into the sails. Slowly, the boat began to move from the dock and gather speed as more wind filled and curved the sails. "Aaron owns the hardware store," Doyle continued. "Dollars to doughnuts he has his wife minding the store while he tries to make it through the bottleneck."

I looked a question, "Bottleneck?" He nodded to the line of rocks far out on the water. "Those rocks, boy. We're in a bay here, see, and it's relatively peaceful. Outside the line of those rocks lies the Atlantic Ocean. It can get mean, I'm telling you! There's a narrow passageway through the rocks to the ocean. That's what we call the bottleneck. Many of us have scraped or hurt our boats trying to sail through it on a windy day. Now that fool Aaron Carmody is trying."

I watched the bright orange sail. It flapped one way then another. I wondered what Aaron Carmody was trying to do. I glanced at Doyle, who was handling the tiller deftly with one hand and taking care of the sail with the other. Catching my eye on him, he explained.

"Think of the *Dragonfly* as a pumpkin seed. If you squeeze the seed between your ıumb and index finger, the seed pops out, right?" I nodded. "All right, now. The main sail is your index finger, your thumb is the center-board. When the wind blows, it exerts a force that would move the boat sideways except that the center-board produces a counter force. So, when the wind blows, the boat moves forward—just like that pumpkin seed."

Doyle paused for a moment, waiting for me to think this through. Then he said, "Now, listen up. When I push the tiller to one side, the boat will move in the opposite direction. When I push the tiller down, that means I push with the wind. The rudder will turn the boat into the wind. When I push the tiller up, like this, it means I want to turn off from the wind."

It looked easy when he did it. Now with the wind

at its back, the boat skimmed the bright water. "Running free," Doyle called it. I waited for the seasickness to begin, but it didn't. Instead, I felt something hard and tight inside me loosen up. The sound of the water whooshing and slap-slapping against the boat was soothing, and so was the flap of the sails above. I leaned up against the side of the *Dragonfly* and fixed my eyes on the sky.

There was a change in the movement of the boat. "Wind's shifting," Doyle explained and kind of smiled at me. The wind and sail noises seemed to have calmed him down too. "See that sail, the upper part?" he asked. "When we're sailing, you just keep an eye on it. If it starts to flutter, the wind's shifted. It can—Watch it!"

As he shouted, the boom swung around and nearly cracked my head open. The *Dragonfly* began to rock violently. "Shift places—quick!" Doyle commanded. I scrambled for my life. He added quite calmly, "That was jibing. You want to watch out for that. When you're running free, even a small, unexpected wind shift can cause an accidental jibe." He maneuvered the boat around, adding, "Now we're going to tack."

We began to zigzag across the water. "Ready about, hard a-lee," Doyle sang out and moved from one side of the boat to the other. "Means we're coming about," he explained. "Watch your head again." I ducked as the boom swung around. "That's it," he said. "You'll get the hang of it. Now, swap places with me and we'll do it again."

I was getting used to moving around the boat. This time when we came about, I ducked almost automatically. As I changed places with Doyle, I noticed that the orange sail was still out there, by the rocks. "Is he having trouble?" I asked.

Doyle grinned. "Aaron always has trouble," he said. "Maybe we'd better go help him out." We shifted course and began to move toward the bright orange sail. As we skimmed along, Doyle suddenly said, "You don't think much of school, is that it?"

Taken by surprise, I just shrugged. He clicked his tongue against his teeth. "Don't keep doing that, boy. Answer."

"Guess not. I'm not good at book stuff."

"But you wrote okay for Rosemary Towers. And I've seen you reading the newspaper, so I guess you know how to read."

"Some. My mom taught me, like I said. There were old newspapers and such around, and I can do up numbers. Used to have a game where I added numbers on the license plates of cars moving past us. But I don't know school junk."

Doyle sighed. "Rob, kids have to go to school till they're sixteen—that's the law." He gave a snort. "Will you look at that, now."

Aaron Carmody's orange sail was slip-sliding through the narrow opening between the rocks. "He's making it through the bottleneck," I said.

"Too early to tell. Winds and currents in that place could easily—" Doyle broke off, frowned. "Dang fool isn't alone. He's got Debbie with him."

Debbie Carmody. I thought of the way she'd looked

at me today in RC32. I felt my face flush and hid it by turning to stare at Aaron's distant, pitching orange sail.

"Smart girl, or so Aaron keeps telling me," Doyle said. "Hear she's so smart she helps out with kids who have trouble learning."

So that was why Debbie Carmody had been in RC32. I turned to look at the orange sail again, then gripped the *Dragonfly*'s edge. "They're going over!" I cried.

"No. Not yet, anyway. But we'd better get out there to help them in case they do."

We stopped running free and turned toward the wind. The *Dragonfly* began to tip on its side, dipping down toward the water. I yelled for Doyle to be careful, but he just laughed. "We call this heeling," he explained. "Don't worry, I can control how far we heel by letting out the sail. Meanwhile, we equalize the position of the boat by balancing it with our weight—what we call hiking out. Come over here and I'll show you."

Me? Hike out? No way. I shook my head, but Doyle paid no attention at all. "I said, move!" he rasped in the same kind of voice he'd used on the big guy, Jason. "Now!"

I moved. Doyle was leaning way out over the edge of the *Dragonfly,* his legs braced, his hands gripping the taut line of the sail. "Over here," Doyle commanded.

I settled my rump on the edge of the boat, braced my feet under the seat, and leaned back. I closed my eyes over the dizzying foam of water. I'd fall in for sure. I'd drown. A sickness began to froth in my stomach, and I knew I must be turning green.

"Move," Doyle commanded.

My insides swooped around and nearly fell out as the boat suddenly seemed to change direction. Now it was almost perpendicular to the water. I could feel cold spume on my face.

"It's heeling. Quick—hike," Doyle shouted. "You too scared, Rob?"

He was enjoying this. I hated him—hated him so much that I forgot how sick I felt. Scared? I was so scared my heart seemed wrapped around my tonsils. But when Doyle hiked out, I tried to balance the boat by doing the same. I was clumsy and slow and my hands were all thumbs, but I did it. I even opened my eyes long enough to glare at Doyle.

He didn't even notice. "Look," he said, nodding across the water. We'd almost caught up to Aaron Carmody and his orange-sailed boat. I could see Debbie clearly now. She was hiking out, while her father, a bald-headed guy with a red face, was bringing the boat around. As we watched, Aaron Carmody shook his head and began to sail his boat away from the bottleneck.

"Giving up, Aaron?" Doyle called. "Not surprised. A bad day to try the bottleneck—too much wind."

"Too much wind, your granny," Aaron shouted back. "Debbie didn't want me to try it, that's all."

Debbie didn't say anything. She smiled at Doyle, but me she totally ignored. "No help needed, then?" Doyle was saying.

"Help? Are you kidding? You're the one who needs help, Kurt, you with your new crew." He suddenly grinned. "What say we race back to the marina?"

Doyle raised his eyebrows, then pulled them down into a frown. He glanced at me. "Think we could try, Rob?"

I started to say no, but hesitated. Debbie. I wanted her to look at me without that disgust. "Why not?" I asked.

For once, Doyle's grin was warm. "Good. But you listen, Rob. There's a strong wind blowing against us, so we'll have to do some fancy sailing to beat even old Aaron Carmody. We can't sail directly against a wind, so we have to tack, see? First we sail to the right, then to the left—sort of inch our way into port. We'll have to do a lot of hiking out. You game?" I nodded again.

"You chickening out, Kurt Doyle?" Aaron roared. His bald head was red with excitement. I saw Debbie getting ready, looking eager and sure of herself. She still didn't look at me.

"Not on your life, Carmody. Get ready. Get set—"

My heart had started to hammer. I did exactly as Doyle told me and held onto the main sheet. "When I tell you to move, be ready," Doyle said.

"Move!"

We moved! Doyle pushed the tiller and the *Dragonfly* surged forward. Doyle laughed as we passed the Carmody boat. "Fool's pinching into the wind," he shouted at me. "We'll beat him easily, Rob. Now, we're going to begin our first tack."

I hardly knew what he was talking about, but I tried to do as he did. A steady wind was blowing out at us from the shore. The *Dragonfly* was heeling really close to the water. I felt dizzy as I hiked out, but forced the sickness down.

Not too far behind us, Aaron Carmody and his orange sail were moving along. I couldn't see his face, but I knew how hard he was trying to catch up. Doyle laughed, grimly. "Aaron's been trying to beat me in a race for years! Never done it, never will. Debbie's a better sailor than he is, even—"

We tacked again, came about, and again the boat heeled. "Hike out!" Doyle shouted at me. "Doing fine, boy! At this rate, we'll wrap it up in no time. Aaron will still be telling it to the sea gulls when we dock and moor the *Dragonfly!*"

I braced my legs and bent backward over the water. The boat moved fast, cutting like a knife through the waves. Again I felt the dizzy sickness grow inside me, fought it. Not now, I told myself. Not now—no! But the sickness grew in me, grew in me . . .

"Rob!"

I heard Doyle's voice shout my name from far off. Next thing I knew, I was in the water. It was filling my eyes, nose, throat—everything. I came up coughing water, spluttering, and saw that the *Dragonfly* was a hundred yards away! I opened my mouth to shout for Doyle, got salt in my mouth. He was leaving me!

I knew he was furious at me. I couldn't blame him. But to leave me out here . . . I thought of sharks and of drowning. The lifejacket around me kept me up, which was a good thing, because the way I felt right then I'd have gone straight to the bottom. Just as I figured I couldn't feel any worse, I did. Aaron and Debbie Carmody's boat went sailing past me—and past Doyle. Both Aaron and Debbie were shouting and waving.

Doyle was coming back for me. He didn't say a word as he helped me out of the water. In total silence we sailed to the marina, and, while I dripped helplessly, Doyle secured the boat and took down the sails.

"You cold?" he asked me. I nodded. I was shaking so hard my teeth were clattering. "There's a blanket in the van. Go on up there and wait for me," Doyle said. "I'll bring the stuff."

He was short with me and I didn't blame him. How could I? I'd let him down. As I wearily climbed the seawall stairs, I heard Pa's voice against my inner ear. Pa told me I was stupid and no-account clumsy, and I agreed with everything he said. I was really miserable, but not as miserable as when I turned back to the quay and saw Aaron Carmody and Debbie shaking hands with Doyle. Aaron would be gloating, I knew, and Debbie—what could she think of me now? I began to wish Doyle hadn't picked me out of the sea after all.

He didn't come up the stairs for a long time. Waiting for him, I sat in the van with the blanket around me and huddled like a sick rat. Finally, Doyle came up the seawall, looking more stoop-shouldered than I'd ever seen him, and threw the sail and tiller into the back of the van. Then he got into the van, started the engine, and gave me a long look.

"Are you all right?" he asked.

"S-s-sure," I stuttered through my shakes. I waited for him to tell me what a deadbeat I was. But, to my surprise, all he did was shake his head.

"Aaron feels ten feet tall," he said, ruefully. He gave this little laugh. "I've been beating him for years now. Stands to reason the man should feel pleased."

I wished he would yell at me, hit me even. "It was my fault you lost," I mumbled.

He blinked at me. "Your fault, Rob? What do you know about boats? It was my big mistake, no two ways around it." He frowned terribly, almost grinding his teeth. "To make you try to race and crew for me on your first day out on the water—what a stupid thing to do!"

I held my breath, waiting for him to explode, not understanding him, afraid. He reached out, and I felt myself cringe back into the seat, readying myself for the blow. What he did was tuck the blanket around me.

"Told Aaron Carmody he'd be hearing from me again," he said to me. Frowning awfully, he nodded. "Yes, sir, next time we'll beat him hollow."

We?

"You did okay for your first time out, Rob," he said. And smiled. "You're all right."

CHAPTER 6

A few days later, the results of my school tests came out at my "core." This meant that Doyle, me, and a bunch of teachers, including Dr. Braun and Mrs. Sidman, met at school. We all got together around this long table in a special room. Mrs. Sidman cleared her throat and said that this meeting was being held so that Doyle and I could see where I fit into the school.

I didn't want to stick around and listen. I figured that zero-minus was where I'd fit in. But there was a surprise. Mrs. Sidman said that the test scores showed I was a pretty smart kid.

"Your IQ places you in the high-average range," she said. "Also, in spite of the fact that you haven't had much formal education, you scored quite well in both math and verbal skills. You speak fairly good English, and, considering your background, your writing isn't bad—except for the spelling."

Smart? Me? My jaw must have dropped a hundred feet, and I could hear Pa's mocking whisper, *They made a mistake. A bad one. You, smart? You're a joke, Rob!*

"We're recommending an easy schedule for you at first," Mrs. Sidman went on. "You'll be carrying four subjects, with two sessions a day in RC32 for support. I'm sure you'll do well, Rob."

"Sure he will," Doyle said. It was the first time he'd opened his mouth, so everybody looked at him, especially me. He got a little red in the face. "The boy's smart," he said, and he gave me a little wink. It felt weird. Doyle was *proud* of me!

Before I could think about that, though, Dr. Braun began to talk about my "low self-image." He said that I also had something called a "self-fulfilling prophecy," which meant that I always failed because I thought I'd fail. Dr. Braun said I had great potential, but no self-confidence, and Doyle frowned in his old way. That made all the good feelings go away.

The core took a long time, nearly an hour. Then, Doyle went home and I was sent to RC32. When I walked in, Debbie Carmody was there. She was helping some kids with math, looking really serious. I wished I had the nerve to join them, but I just hung around the door, waiting till Mr. Fitz saw me and motioned me over to another corner of the room.

"I heard things went well in the testing," he said, and he smiled to show me he wasn't holding the other day's incident against me. "Learn well, Robby, and you'll be out of here in no time. I know what some kids call this room, but I want you to know that the real dummies are the ones who don't know what goes on in here!" He nodded to Debbie. "Deb's the smartest kid in her class, but because she had a reading problem, a learning disability, she didn't realize how smart she was. She came to us for a while and look at her now."

At the sound of her name, Debbie looked at us, and then away. Even if Mr. Fitz was forgetting and forgiving, Debbie wasn't! When Mr. Fitz suggested she come over and help me with some word problems, she shook her head.

"Not right now," she said. "As soon as I finish over here, okay?"

I felt the turndown, even though Mr. Fitz didn't. He worked with me for a while, though, and then left me to figure out the problems on my own. Seth and Dan drifted in and gave me the high sign. I pretended not to see, but Seth came right over. "You shouldn't work so hard, man," he said. "You'll give the Dummy Room a bad rep."

"Don't you call it that, Seth Boudine!"

We both turned. Debbie Carmody was watching us. She was red-cheeked and angry.

"What's eating you?" Seth drawled.

"You're the dummy, coming here and making cracks. You're so lazy you don't study and pass your subjects. If you can't say anything half decent, at least shut up and stop bugging people."

She turned away with a whirl of dark hair and began helping the kids again. Seth made a rude noise.

"Debbie thinks she's better than anyone else," Dan said, spitefully.

Debbie didn't turn around, but I saw her neck muscles tighten. I wanted to leave those two guys and walk over to her, but Seth and Dan were standing beside me. I couldn't move without tangling with one of them. And to make things worse, when Mr. Fitz told me to sit down and work, they sat on either side of me.

"Heard about you," Seth whispered. "I mean, heard what *really* happened to you, man. Running away and having to live with old man Doyle."

Dan added, "Jason says that Doyle used to be a hard-nosed cop." The name brought back the memory of the dark-bearded guy with the gray eyes. I remembered how mad Doyle had looked the day we met up with Jason.

"Who's Jason?" I asked.

"A really cool dude." Seth's voice had respect in it. He nudged me. "Tell us about it. I mean, living on your own. I bet you could tell us some stuff."

I wanted to say being alone is no fun; it's not great, and it's not glamorous, so get that fantasy out of your head. But Mr. Fitz was glaring at us, so I said, "Later." They nodded. I told myself that if I possibly could, I'd lose them "later." Seth and Dan were bad news, and I didn't want any part of them.

It was easier than I'd thought to lose them. My English teacher, Mr. Lind, kept me after school that day so that he could help me with a poem the kids had been working on. It was a poem by this guy Kipling, and though I couldn't understand all the words, I somehow got the feel of it. That's what Mr. Lind said, anyway.

"You have a feel for words, Rob," he said, perching on his desk and watching me. "You like words, don't you?"

I shrugged, not knowing what he meant by that.

English class was killing me. I didn't know beans about grammar, and my spelling was something from outer space, and here Mr. Lind was talking about my liking words! By the time he let me out of his classroom, my head felt like it was packed with cotton balls.

I decided to walk rather than wait for the late bus. I wanted to clear my head, and the walk home was by the seawall and easy to follow. It was a fine day with high silky clouds, and as I came nearer the seawall I could smell the sea. I was taking deep breaths of it when I saw that someone else had decided to walk. Someone was standing on top of the seawall, and by the way her hair blew back dark and straight, I knew it was Debbie Carmody.

I stopped, then gave myself a shake. Hey, it was my sea as much as it was hers! Without even looking at Debbie, I climbed up the steps to the top of the wall. From there I could see breakers with their white tops throwing themselves against the sand. In the distance, foam was slashing against the bottleneck. A big sea gull, mewing in the funny way sea gulls do, swooped down. There was the salt and the cold smell of seaweed.

"Why are you following me?"

I turned my head and saw Debbie had whipped around to glare at me.

"I wasn't following you!"

She had a fist planted on each hip. "No fooling? Well, you and your creepy pals can follow me from here to China, and I'll still have nothing to do with you!"

"I didn't follow you," I repeated. Her eyes were

sort of gray-green, like the sea. She was so mad her freckles were rose-colored.

She whirled around and stomped away from me across the top of the seawall. I watched her go and made myself turn back to the ocean. Right away a well-known voice started whispering at me. *Well? What did you expect, boy? You are dirt. Always will be dirt . . .*

Something brushed my arm. I looked sideways, saw Debbie standing there. She had her hand upraised, uncertain, as if she'd touched my shoulder then pulled back. "I'm sorry," she said, voice unsure, too. "I shouldn't have jumped on you like that. I know you're new to Laysner and the school and everything. But Seth and Dan are bad news, and so are their friends."

"I'm not their friend," I mumbled.

She didn't answer that, but took a deep breath. "Isn't the ocean great?" she asked.

"It's okay, I guess."

"Okay? Mister, you are nuts. It is fabulous, terrific, wonderful, marvelous, and super!"

I laughed, and she grinned. "You sound like a dictionary," I told her.

"That's what my folks say. You know, when I first went to RC32, I had trouble reading. I mixed letters and numbers up. Now I'm learning to work around it." She gave me this look. "I heard what Mr. Fitz said to you about trouble with your English class. If you'd like, I'll help you."

She started walking down the stairs cut into the seawall and I followed. We walked out on the narrow stretch of sand between us and the sea. "Hey, can you skip pebbles?" she asked.

Could I skip pebbles! There'd been this kid in Louisiana who showed me how. I skipped a couple for Debbie. She opened her green eyes real wide and said, "Wow!"

My words came out in a rush. "I could teach you," I said. "I could teach you and you could help me with English. Like a trade."

She hesitated, and I thought, I've been dumb again, I've loused up again. Then she smiled. "Why not? Skipping for Kipling. It rhymes, kind of." I asked her how she knew about the Kipling, and she shrugged. "You have Mr. Lind, don't you? He likes that kind of stuff. I had Kipling's poems when I was in his class."

We walked, kicking up the damp sand and picking up shells that were gritty and wet. It seemed like a short time before Debbie was pointing. "That's where we have to climb back up," she told me. "The town's right around the corner from there." As we began to climb the stone steps she added, "I'm going to Dad's store for a while. Want to come?"

"I guess so," I said. "Why not?"

I was feeling good and also a little afraid of feeling so good. I followed Debbie up the stone steps, down onto the winding road, and on to Main. As we came into sight of the sign that said "Carmody's Hardware," Debbie asked, "So, are you getting along with Kurt Doyle?"

"I guess," I said.

"Laysner is a small town, so everybody knows what everybody else is doing," Debbie explained. "Kurt Doyle has lived alone for a long time, and then suddenly you come along. All the women started to gossip, and the men were worse than the women. Dad heard a lot of what they said in his hardware store."

I could just picture Aaron Carmody, with his red face and reddening bald head, listening. "What did he hear?" I asked. My insides knotted up as Debbie told me my own story.

"Dad said you were a ward of the state and that your father went away and left you," she reported. It sounded so cold, said out like that. I shrugged. "Isn't that the way it was?" Debbie asked, curious.

"He didn't want to go," I said. "He . . . he had to."

"Why?" Debbie asked. "I can't see my father doing that."

I looked at her and saw she was looking at me in a puzzled way. How could Debbie understand? Like Doyle said, she was an only child. Her folks probably let her do anything she wanted, gave her everything she asked for.

"He had to find work," I found myself saying. "Mom died, see, and . . . and it was the only thing he could do. He tried to take care of me, but he couldn't do it."

Debbie frowned. "But why would he just leave you?" she asked, slowly.

"The state took me away. Figured a single man couldn't handle a kid."

"So they gave you to Kurt Doyle?" Good question, that. Boy, was I dumb!

"Personal reasons," I said, stiffly. "They're not things I'd tell everybody, but . . . he was sick." Her eyes widened, and I thought quickly. "TB."

She shook her head sorrowfully, and I saw a kind of mist come into her gray-green eyes. "I'm sorry," she said quietly. "I shouldn't have been so nosy. I won't tell anyone, Rob, I mean it."

I felt crummy. But what else could I have told her? Could I have said, Look, Deb, my father is a drunk who beat me up whenever he wanted to, and then washed his hands of me?

"He didn't want to leave me," I heard myself say. "He cried when they told him. We both did. He said, 'I'll come back for you some day, Rob.' " Debbie was still watching me, so I added, "He said, 'You are my whole life.' "

"That's so sad!" Debbie looked ready to cry, too. She grabbed my hand. "Oh, he'll be back. I know he will!"

We'd come to Carmody's Hardware now, and I could see Mr. Carmody himself out in front, talking to a departing customer. He saw us coming and smiled at Debbie.

"Well, look whose bad penny showed up," he said. The words were an insult, but the way he said them made it sound a lot different. I watched Debbie walk over to her father, and deep inside me I knew that if Pa had ever looked at me like that or spoken to me like that just once, I'd never have asked for another thing.

"Hey, Rob!" a familiar voice called, and I saw Seth Boudine and his fat sidekick walking toward the hardware store. With them was the black-bearded guy, Jason. All of them were heading right for me.

CHAPTER 7

I thought, if I ignore them, they'll go away. I turned my back on them, and Dan snickered, "Hey, maybe Rob doesn't want to see us. He's with his girlfriend!"

I felt my face flame. I started to follow Debbie up the steps, but all of a sudden, Seth had cut me off. "We just want to be friendly," he said, with this nasty little smile. "Hey, there's going to be a party at my house tonight. Want to come?"

Nobody had ever asked me to a party before. I hesitated for just a minute, when Mr. Carmody's loud voice broke in. "You boys! Get out of here!" he cried.

It was the wrong thing to say. I felt myself slowly go hot, then cold. Jason hooked his big thumbs in the belt of his jeans. "You don't tell us to go nowhere," he said in his deep voice. "We're minding our business. It's a free country."

"Yeah," Dan said impudently. He moved closer to Mr. Carmody, who was getting redder by the minute. Then he shoved past Debbie's father and into the store. "We're customers, man!"

Seth followed. Mr. Carmody looked like he wanted to stop them, but he glanced at Jason and hesitated. Jason was smiling, his hands still hooked into his belt. "Just helping the economy go round, Mr. Carmody," he said.

Mr. Carmody made a noise in his throat and ducked into the store after Seth and Dan. Debbie looked upset and angry. "Rob," she whispered, "we've got to do something. Those two can cause all kinds of damage . . ."

Do? What did she expect me to do? Her own father couldn't stand up to Jason! As if he were reading my mind, Jason turned his grin on me. "Tell Doyle I was asking about his health," he said nastily. "Tell him the streets aren't the same without him."

Suddenly there was this sound of things falling, and Mr. Carmody let out a yell. Debbie dashed into the hardware store with me right behind her. A big box of nails had been dumped all over the floor, and Dan stood nearby while Mr. Carmody practically danced up and down.

"Pick them up!" he was shrieking. "You pick them up, you riffraff!"

"It was an accident," Dan said. He nudged Seth. "So sue me."

Mr. Carmody made a lunge at Dan, and Dan skipped backward, banging into another box. Its contents spilled all over. Seth shouted with laughter and kicked the stuff around.

"I'm calling the police," Debbie said. She was really pale, and her eyes were like an angry cat's. She headed for the phone behind the store counter, but the guys had had enough. With a final kick at the stuff on the floor, Seth sauntered out the door, Dan behind him. Outside, I heard Jason's loud laughter.

All of a sudden, it was really quiet in the hardware store. Mr. Carmody just stood there looking at the mess on the floor. "Dad, shall I call the police?" Debbie asked, talking in a low voice.

He shook his head. "They'd just claim it was an accident . . ." He got down on his hands and knees and started to pick up the stuff. I started to help him, but he glared at me. "You! You're one of their friends, aren't you?" He was getting ready to throw me out, when Debbie stepped in.

"Dad, no! This is Robby!" She said. "He lives with Kurt Doyle."

The red had begun to leave Mr. Carmody's face, but he didn't look too pleased to have me there. "So you're the one," he growled, and he gave Debbie this worried look. "You and Debbie have a lot of classes together?"

I said no, and he looked relieved. You could read Mr. Carmody's thoughts as plain as any newspaper. He didn't want someone like me, a ward of the state, a runaway kid who'd tried to kill himself, getting too friendly with his daughter. He made that even plainer by turning his back on me. He ignored me so totally that I got up without picking up any more stuff and told Debbie that I had to go.

She followed me out onto the step. "Don't be upset with Dad," she said. "He's not mad at you." I nodded. "Remember, we have a deal. Kipling for skipping." She glanced up and down the street. "I guess they're gone, Dan and Seth and that creep Jason."

I asked Debbie who Jason was, and she said he was some kind of local hood. "He really gets into everything, but the police can't prove he did anything," she told me. "I guess long ago he and Kurt Doyle had some run-ins. Jason likes to rile him whenever he sees him, now that Mr. Doyle's retired from the police force."

I wondered whether I should give Doyle the message Jason had given me to deliver, but before I could say any more to Debbie, her father shouted for her to be quick and come help him. "Don't stand there all day talking to—" He bit off the words, but I knew what he was thinking. He didn't want her to be talking to a loser.

I started to walk to Doyle's, and the day didn't seem so bright any more. In a way I couldn't blame Mr. Carmody. He'd lumped me together with Seth and Dan and Jason. I couldn't blame him, but by the time I'd reached the house, I felt so low that even Elmer couldn't cheer me up. He licked my hand, and when I hunkered down, he tried to get up on his hind legs to lick my cheek.

I put my arms around his fat doggyness and gave him a little hug and shake. For some reason, I wanted to hold onto something right then—to hold on tight. "Mr. Carmody looked at me like folks always looked at me and Pa," I whispered to Elmer. "Like we were dirt."

Elmer whined. He wanted me to turn him loose, but I needed to hang onto him.

"When I was with Pa, I felt like dirt," I told Elmer. "Pa told me so all the time. He was mean when he was drunk and meaner when he was sober. Man, Elmer, I saw it all—drunk tanks and not having anything to eat except soda and Cheerios for a week and never being able to wash. And the places we lived in stank . . ."

I pushed my face into the soft, silky, good-smelling doggy coat and Elmer turned to lick my ear. It tickled. "Will you cut that out?"

"He likes the salt taste on you," Doyle's voice behind me said. I dropped Elmer and jumped up to see him standing in the doorway watching me. How long had he been listening? Had he heard everything I said?

"You're early," I said.

"So I am. Thought we'd take the *Dragonfly* for a spin, if you felt like it. Nothing like the good sea air to clear out the cobwebs." He stopped a moment, staring at me. "And, Rob . . ."

I waited, but all he said was to take an extra sweater or something; it was chilly outside. "Be chillier on the water, even," he added. "Don't want anything to happen to you, boy."

Next day, I told Debbie about the sailing. "It was really windy," I told her. "Nearly capsized us twice, but Kurt managed to keep floating."

She sighed. "Kurt Doyle is the best sailor in Laysner. I've always wanted him to take me out in the *Dragonfly*."

"Maybe sometime when I learn how, I can take you out," I said. The minute the words were out I wanted to call them back, but Debbie just nodded. "Doyle says I sail really good for a beginner," I went on, quickly. "He's been giving me lessons."

Debbie gave me a quick look through those long-lashed green eyes. "I'd like that," she said and smiled.

I walked into my first class on air, and not even English got me down. Debbie had helped me with it, before school, explained the Kipling poem we had to learn. It was a really long poem, and when I looked at it, it scared me, but Debbie had told me it was easy. So when the teacher asked the class if anybody could explain it, up went my hand.

"The poem 'If' is kind of a man's advice to his son," I told the class. "He always starts his advice off with 'if.' If some people blame you for something that's not your fault, keep your head cool and work it out. Stuff like that. I guess."

"Very good, Rob," Mr. Lind said, and I sensed his pleasure. That made me feel even better. He knew I was trying, and he seemed to like me. Later on in the period, he told me to take some records back to the library for him. "You might as well get used to your school," he added, smiling.

So, pleased with myself, I walked out of the classroom and delivered the records to the library. On the way back I saw Seth and Dan.

They were near the lav where the tough kids usually hung out. "Hey, look," Dan piped up, "it's the dork."

I tried to ignore him, but Seth stuck out an arm and stopped me. He had thick, muscled arms, powerful enough to belt me into next week if he wanted. "You mad at us or something?" he wanted to know. "You keep ignoring us. Too good for us, maybe?"

"Get off my case," I told him.

"You're no prize, Rob Holland. And your father's a drunken bum—"

My hands fisted tightly, but I kept my temper. Seth wanted me to try something. "You're chicken," he said, coldly and with disgust. "You're a loser, so you'll do what I say or else."

In my ear, Pa's voice rang. *So how come he got your number so fast, Rob? You're everything he says. You're dirt. Think you're so high and mighty because Doyle lets you in his boat? Because you understood that stinking poem?*

"I have to go back to class," I said, and hated the whispery way my voice came out. "Just leave me alone, okay?"

"Sure, sure, after you have a smoke with us," Dan grinned.

"I don't smo—"

Seth didn't hit me, but he caught hold of me and shook me so hard I swallowed the word. "Sure you do," he crooned. "You'll do anything we tell you to do, wimp."

They dragged me back into the lav, and Dan lit up a cigarette. He pulled on it and passed it to Seth, who kept his pale eyes on me while he drew in the smoke. "Here," he snapped and watched as I pulled in smoke and nearly choked. "Again," Seth ordered.

My lungs felt seared. I was sick. For a second I thought of throwing up all over Seth, but I knew that if

I did that, he'd kill me. I *was* going to be sick the next time I had to smoke that thing, but luckily Seth's interest was wavering.

"This place is a damned morgue," he complained, "it's so boring. I've been kicked out of two classes already today, and I have ninety-nine days of detention coming."

"Let's do something," Dan suggested. I saw a light coming into Seth's pale eyes. He nodded. "What'll we do?" Dan asked.

"You'll see." Keeping hold of me, Seth dragged me into the hallway. He turned the corner from the lav, pointed to the fire alarm.

"Are you crazy?" I gasped. "You can't pull that."

He grinned at me. "We're not going to do it, dork-face. You are."

I told him, no way. Seth pulled my arm behind me in a hammerlock and pushed down.

"You're crazy," I half-sobbed. The pain was so awful I felt sicker than before. Seth gave my arm one more squeeze and then let me go.

"Aah, he'd do it wrong, anyway. Keep a lookout, Dan."

Dan kept watch while Seth approached the alarm box. Seth looked both ways and took a deep breath. Suddenly he smacked the glass of the box with his elbow. Glass went all over.

"You say anything, Rob, you're dead," he warned. His pale eyes were glittering with excitement. "Now, run like hell—"

He grabbed the lever in the box and pulled. Hard. I

started to say "No!" then realized I was free and could move. I took off down the hall as the biggest, noisiest sound I'd ever heard started up behind me. I glanced over my shoulder and saw Seth and Dan taking off and running. The noise buzzed and squawked and bleeped behind me.

"Fire!" I heard somebody shout. A classroom door to my left flew open. The kids came out in a row, hurrying and pushing, the teacher right behind them, trying to keep order. One little kid fell to his knees right in front of me. It was that pale kid I'd seen in RC32 the first day of school. I helped him up.

"It's not a drill . . . it's a real fire," he gasped. "Or else a bomb scare . . ."

"Keep moving!" the teacher behind us called. He looked pale, too. "Keep moving!"

I knew I should find my English class, but I didn't dare. All around me, streams of kids were pouring out of classes, hurrying down corridors to exits. "Keep in single file! Don't push! Walk directly to the fire exit!" teachers kept shouting.

The line I was in turned, went through swinging doors and into the sunshine beyond. "Gee, a real fire . . . Naw, a bomb scare, that's all! Listen, hear the fire engines . . ."

They came wailing out of the distance. I could hear the firemen shouting instructions at each other. I wondered where Seth and Dan had got to and felt a sick taste in my mouth. I wished I had the guts to shout out that it was a false alarm, that Dan and Seth had done it. But I didn't dare.

We stood outside for a long time, and then the principal came to the doorway and told us it was all right. "There's no fire," he said in a harassed voice. "Someone pulled the fire alarm in the 400s wing." His eyes swept us all. "Whoever did this was not only stupid and immature, but also broke the law. There's a stiff penalty for setting off a false alarm!"

We shuffled back to class just as the period buzzer sounded. I went to my next class, math, and the kids were all talking about the false alarm. Ten minutes into the period the squawk box announced that Robert Holland should go to the office—the principal wanted to talk to him.

My heart started banging. Had anyone seen me running down the 400s wing? My mouth dry, I walked through the empty corridor were the janitor was sweeping up bits of glass from the alarm. "Lousy kids," he was muttering. I couldn't blame him, but it started me shaking again, shaking like I couldn't stop. Why? I asked myself. I hadn't done anything! But the janitor's muttering had become Pa's voice again: *Lousy jerk. Creep. Can't do anything right. What right did you have being born, Rob Holland?*

I jammed my fists into my pockets as I walked into the office. They sent me right into the principal's little cubicle. "Sit down," he told me. "I'm talking to all the students who were seen in the 400s wing around the time of the alarm. I hear you were in the library just before the alarm went off, and the library is near the 400s wing." He paused, eyes glinting at me. "Did you see or hear anything, Rob?"

I really wanted to tell him about Dan and Seth. Why should I shield those two creeps? I was scared, that was why! "I didn't see anything," I muttered.

"Whoever did this did a dumb thing. Have you ever seen a real fire, Rob?"

"Once," I said, "in Louisiana." I remembered the fire department coming to this house while people watched their home burn. The people had screamed and cried, and the fire had raged while smoke made everyone choke and cough.

"A false alarm wastes dollars and time. If you do know anything, it's your duty to speak up."

I squeezed my fists tight and gasped as I felt the pain. The principal stared at my hand. "Where did you hurt your hand?" he asked.

"My . . . hand?" I opened my fist, saw a drop of blood. I frowned, then remembered—the cut glass. "I guess I cut it," I mumbled.

"There was glass all around the fire alarm box, wasn't there?" His eyes were knowing, like he was a detective who'd just figured out the mystery.

I didn't know what to say. I hung my head, bit my lip. "I guess," I finally said. "I don't know about that."

He looked at me a long, long time. Then he said, soft and nasty, "I heard that you and Seth Boudine and Dan Evanson hang around together. If one of you knows about this, has done this, you'll be sorry. Remember you've got to answer to the state for whatever you do, Rob."

I was shaking so hard I knew he could see me tremble. "Can I go now?"

He nodded, reluctantly, then gave a little disgusted motion with his hand. "Get out," he said.

I had almost walked out of his office when he called me back. "Robert, it's against school rules to smoke in school. You stink like a tobacco factory," he said. He stabbed a finger at me. "It makes me sick, thinking how much a man like Kurt Doyle is going through for you! Here you are, using the taxpayers' money, going to school, while all the time you're laughing up your sleeve and breaking every law you can. I just want you to know one thing. Sooner or later, we'll find you out. We'll see what you're really like."

CHAPTER 8

The news that I'd been called down to the principal's office spread like wildfire. Most kids in school figured that Seth and Dan had done it as usual, but a few felt that I'd been involved. I was afraid of what Debbie might think, but she only smiled and said it was like in the poem.

"Remember? 'If you can keep your head when all around you, people are losing theirs and blaming you' . . ." she told me. That cheered me up. So did Doyle's reaction to the whole thing.

"If you say you didn't do it, you didn't," he rasped at me when I told him what had happened. He looked at me closely. "So you got blamed for something you didn't do?" I shrugged. "And it bothers you." He hesitated, nodded. "Right. Only place to lose bad feelings is out there on the water."

So we went sailing, and Doyle taught me more about handling the *Dragonfly,* even let me sail a little while he watched. It was funny. We didn't talk much while we were out on the water, but I felt a lot more comfortable there with Doyle than I did anywhere else. My hands, usually clumsy and unsure, seemed to take to the boat right away. Doyle said I was a born sailor.

"Got seawater in your veins," he said. "Never knew a kid who took to it so fast."

I wondered if Doyle had taken his daughter sailing with him, but I didn't ask. It didn't seem to matter. Nothing mattered out on the sea but the sound of the wind and the flap of the sail and the way the *Dragonfly* handled the waves and the water.

We did a lot of sailing that first month I was with Doyle. It was somehow the answer to everything. When something bugged me at school, we went sailing. If Doyle was cranky about something else, we took the *Dragonfly* out. Sometimes we didn't say a word from the unmooring to the docking. Sometimes he was so quiet I even forgot he was there. Other times we'd talk a little—about the days when he was on the force, things he'd done, good or sad or funny things. One time I asked him about Jason, and he got that angry look in his eyes.

"Jason," he said, "is trash. He knows what I think of him. He's mixed up with a lot of rotten things around here, but he's clever. Someday, maybe, I'll be able to pin something on him." He broke off and smiled a little. "Once a cop, always a cop, I guess."

But his smile was bitter, and though his explanation made sense, I didn't know whether I bought all of it. By now I'd begun to read Doyle pretty well, and I had the feeling he was keeping something back. Something about Jason upset him badly, but not just for the reasons he'd given me.

Another time when we were in the boat, he got me talking about Pa. I started by telling him about the time Pa bought an old junkheap of a car that died in the middle of a long, deserted highway between Alamogordo and White Sands, New Mexico. Then I told Doyle about José, a kid I'd known while we were still in New Mexico, and how José had taken me home to meet his family and eat his mother's cooking.

"They were pickers like us, but they were happy, you know. They sang a lot. José's baby sister's name was Celestina." I grinned, remembering that chubby baby. They taught me some Spanish words and they'd laugh when I tried to pronounce them."

"And you didn't mind their laughing?" Doyle asked me.

"No. It was friendly laughing. They didn't laugh to hurt me, not like—" I stopped. He waited. "Not like Pa."

There was a silence in the boat. The wind whooshed against the sails, making them flap. "Ease off, find the true course again," Doyle instructed me, and I followed his directions. "So your Pa liked to laugh at you," he said.

I nodded. In the sea and wind sounds I could hear Pa's laughing. "He figured it was funny I was clumsy," I said.

"You're not clumsy. Nobody born clumsy could sail a boat. Needs a light and clever hand."

He kept watching me, and I found I was sweating. I didn't want to talk about Pa, but something was squeezing, as if I were a tube of toothpaste, and somehow I needed to get all the hurt and the words squeezed out. "He . . . found out about my going to see José," I finally said. "He got real mad. Called them a bunch of wetbacks. I don't want to talk about it."

We drifted into silence. "You can start soloing pretty soon," Doyle finally said. I blinked at him. "No, I mean it. Only way to sail is all by yourself, sometimes. Not much of a wind today, but you could get some pretty brisk speed out of the old *Fly*. Want to try it?"

"You mean on my own?" I asked.

He grinned. "Sure I mean that. Scare you?"

"No way!" I shouted. Thoughts of Pa and everything else disappeared from my mind. Doyle ordered me to dock, and when we reached the marina he got out. "I'm going to stand right here and watch you," he told me. "Hug the shoreline at first. Feel the right wind before you head out any. Don't go too far and come back when I wave my jacket at you. Got that?"

"Aye, captain," I said. The wind sounded like it was singing to me, and my heart was smashing against my ribs.

He waved me off. I steered away from the dock and into the open water. The sails filled with a deep breath of wind, and I set my course. Soon, I was running free across the bay.

At first, I was cautious. It was as though I could hear Doyle's voice advising me as I sailed. I could see him standing on the shore, hands on hips, watching me. I was scared I wasn't doing it right at first, but soon I quit being scared. I let myself go. I ran free for a while, then turned a hundred eighty degrees and started to tack against the wind. I sang songs José had taught me, and I felt *good.* I felt wonderful and free!

"Who's not a chicken or a wimp or a creep?" I shouted into the water and the wind. "Who's the captain of the *Dragonfly?*" The wind answered me, and the water lapped and splashed and whapped against the boat's sides. "I . . . Robert Holland . . . I . . . am . . . great!"

I didn't realize how far out I was getting till I glanced back at the shore and saw Doyle waving his jacket madly. How long had he been waving it? He looked small and far away, and my good feelings suddenly shriveled up and died inside me. I glanced over my shoulder and saw what I'd been too busy to notice—the dark teeth of the bottleneck were not too far away.

I had to bring the boat around—and quick! It wasn't easy to do. The wind had shifted, and it was blowing out toward the open ocean. "Okay, Rob, stay calm," I told myself. "Get your head together and do it now!"

I tried to head toward the shore, but the wind was too strong for the kind of tacking I was used to. The best I could do was to make short hitches, crawling across the bay like a drunken crab. I had covered half the distance between me and the dock when a tremendous gust of wind caught the sails. I pulled the sails in, felt the boat start to heel. Panicking, I hiked out as far as I could, trying to stabilize the *Dragonfly* with my weight. It didn't work.

I felt the boat start to tip over. Panic wasn't a word for what I felt. In that second I thought frantically what I could do. I thought of Doyle watching me from shore, how he'd trusted me with his precious boat. I thought, please, not now! Then the cold water sucked me under. As the boat turned over, I gasped. Then I swam up to the surface, swam to the boat, and grabbed its side.

I kept thinking, oh, no . . . oh, no! over and over. I knew I was starting to babble to myself. I heard somebody sobbing. It was me. Inside my head, Pa began to tell me off like he usually did. But, shoving Pa aside, I heard another remembered voice. "In case of capsize, follow the regular capsize procedure, Rob. You know what to do."

Right away, I could think again. I was still plenty scared, but I felt steadier. I knew what had to be done. Doyle and I had gone over the procedures together so often that I could repeat them in my sleep. I said the words out loud to pull my nerve together. "In case of capsize, stay with the boat . . ."

I kept saying that to myself as I swam around the *Dragonfly.* She looked so sad, her sails sweeping the water, her proud, red-lined body tipped into the bay. If there were two men, one could hold onto the centerboard to stabilize the boat, I knew. The other would pull down the sail. Then, both would lean on the centerboard and grab the gunwales and heave back into the water as the boat sprang up.

That was how Doyle had taught me. The trouble was, I was only one man.

I took a desperate look at the shore. Doyle was just standing there. Believe it or not, that gave me confidence. If he didn't think I could do this, he'd have been running for help! I pulled myself out of the water and crawled on top of the centerboard. The boat rocked. I leaned back on the sail rope, praying hard. If the wind caught the sails again, it could capsize the boat right on top of me, and there'd be no way I could prevent it from turtling.

Heave . . . heave . . . suddenly the *Dragonfly* snapped up!

For a second I felt such relief that I could have danced and sung. But I realized that my troubles weren't over. The wind was still blowing hard against me. The *Dragonfly* could turn over again. I started to bail, talking to myself like Doyle would have talked to me. "Bail quick, Rob!" and "You've got to reduce sail. You can't go into the eye of the wind and stop dead. Swing the *Dragonfly* onto a true course. Now, bail!"

I bailed. Man, did I bail! As I started to steer, I kept my eye on the shoreline. Doyle just stood there, a dark spot that grew bigger and bigger. He didn't move; he just waited.

I figured he was too furious to move. I'd done a dumb thing, forgetting the rules, taking the *Dragonfly* out too far, and then coming in so quickly I'd capsized the boat. I hated to think of what Doyle would say to me when I got in. The least he'd say was that I could never sail the boat solo again.

But when I sailed into the dock, he didn't seem mad. He didn't say much as I docked the *Dragonfly* and moored it, then started to take down the sails. His silence worried me. Finally, he said, "Rob."

I had to turn around and face him. I had to. He was smiling! "Cold?" He asked me. Unable to speak, I just nodded. "Saw you flapping around out there trying to get the *Dragonfly* back up. Here, I'll get the tiller. You get yourself into that van and wrap up in the blanket."

"I didn't mean to do it." The words came in a rush.

"I sort of figured that. Nobody likes to fall into the ocean and capsize his boat in this wind. Wind came up sudden, didn't it? I wouldn't have let you solo if I'd known." We began to walk to the seawall, Doyle still talking. "I had an anxious moment when you went under, but as soon as I saw you doing the right things, I wasn't worried any more."

A warmth had begun to balloon through me. Doyle wasn't mad at me. Pa's voice, which had begun to sound off inside my head again, went quiet. "It was still dumb to try and tack like that," I said.

"There's a difference between being dumb and being inexperienced." Doyle put his hand on my shoulder. His grip was warm and sure. "Next time we're out, I'll show you how to do it. You'll learn, Rob." As we came up to the old van, he said it. He said, "I'm proud of you."

CHAPTER 9

We fell into a routine. When Doyle wasn't working nights I'd get back from school, start some dinner for us, get Elmer walked, and feed him his dog food plus a piece of cinnamon toast. Then I'd get out the boating equipment and wait for the old van to come tooting up the road.

Doyle would change while I got the stuff loaded into the van, and then we'd make it down to the marina. We timed ourselves. Each day we managed to shave a few seconds off the clock. We also started counting the minutes it took to get the *Dragonfly* ready and running free—minutes and seconds.

As the late spring brought out fine sunsets, we'd take turns sailing and we'd talk, or just drift and watch the sun glide down under the bay. I told Doyle an old Indian legend about sunsets that José had taught me, and he told me about sailing superstitions. Said that sailors didn't like to whistle on or near a boat, because that meant "whistling up a wind." Told me that some sailors were so superstitious they wouldn't even paint a boat blue, because they thought blue brought bad luck. I asked why blue, but Doyle didn't know.

He also told me it was supposed to be bad luck to bring a woman on board a boat. "And that's nonsense," he added. "Lots of women sail and sail well, too."

"Like Debbie Carmody," I said, and he agreed. "She sails better than her father." Doyle nodded again and I watched him, wondering if I could sneak up a proposition on him. I'd been thinking about it for a week, and this seemed a good time. "I was wondering if I could take her sailing sometime," I said.

He gave me this shrewd look. "You mean on the *Dragonfly?* What makes you think you're a good enough sailor?"

"You said I was good," I pointed out.

He said I had plenty to learn. "And I can't see Aaron entrusting his only chick and child to you in a boat," he went on. "For once, he'd probably be right. You need more practice, boy."

I was exasperated. "You say I can sail good!"

"Well," he corrected, "and I'll tell you when well is good enough."

So we kept up the routine, sailing together every few days after school. On the nights when Doyle worked at the warehouse, I studied, played with Elmer, or took a walk. Usually, I'd walk or jog along the seawall. I didn't like going into town, because Seth and Dan hung out there, and I didn't want to get mixed up with them again.

One time, though, I got bored with the seawall and went into town. Nothing was happening, so I decided to walk down the long road from town to Doyle's warehouse. It was only a couple of miles away from the center of town, but the road was so quiet and the warehouse so isolated, you could swear it was hundreds of miles away from anything.

The first time I went to the warehouse, Doyle was worried. He figured that something was wrong at home. When he realized I was just out walking, though, his face relaxed.

"Got the walkies, have you?" he asked me. "I'm glad you came by," he added. "Things are real quiet tonight."

He couldn't talk to me much. He had his rounds to make and the clock to punch. But he seemed so glad to see me I went back other times. That time, Doyle introduced me to his boss, Mr. Jim Fosse, who said I could come whenever I liked, as long as I didn't mess up Doyle's guard duties.

Sometimes I'd take his dinner to him, and we'd sit and talk, listening to the frogs in the nearby swamp. In the darkness it seemed that we could talk more easily, and Doyle even told me a bit about Alma. I figured from what he said, and didn't say, that she was pretty, stubborn, and smart. He never went into why she left home, just said that she had gotten in with the wrong crowd. I knew that he wasn't going to tell me any more than that, knew he kept his thoughts and feelings about Alma deep inside him and hid them even from himself. I knew all about those kinds of feelings.

As spring slid into early summer, my own dark loneliness came less and less often. Pa's sneering voice was pretty near always quiet those days. Sometimes, though, he'd come to me in dreams, head held down like a bull ready to charge, eyes mean and spoiling for a fight. In dreams he still could make me feel two inches tall and no-account, but when I woke up Doyle was there.

Report-card time came, and my first-quarter grades weren't all that bad. "Three C's and a B," Doyle said, looking over the card. "Not bad, Rob."

"It could have been better. I should have got an A in math," I said.

"Doesn't mean you can't do better next time, but you're holding your own right now," Doyle said.

Since he was so pleased with me, I thought I'd try him again about sailing the *Dragonfly.* "I'd like to have the boat this weekend," I began, real matter-of-fact. "You know, leave early and take a picnic lunch . . ."

He cocked his head at me so that his white hair spilled on one side. "I have a hunch you're not inviting me along," he said. "That means someone else is going to share the picnic lunch. Debbie Carmody?" I nodded. "She helped you pass English, so I supposed she's entitled," he then said. "Go ahead."

I said, "Go ahead?"

He pretended to glare at me. "School teaching you to echo, boy? That's what I said. Now, get lost before I come to my senses!"

I ran over to him and hugged him. I don't know who was more surprised, he or I. I stared at him for a second, arms around him. He frowned a little and moved his lips soundlessly, and I dropped my arms. "Go call her," he said, gruffly, and went out of the house and stamped into the yard.

I went to the phone and picked up the receiver, looking out into the yard where Doyle stood gazing out to sea, his hands jammed into his pockets. I dialed Debbie's number and wondered what I was going to say to her.

It was crazy. I could talk to her a mile a minute at school, but now I was tongue-tied. I couldn't even remember my own name. I started to hang up, but it was too late. She was on the phone. "Uh, Debbie?" I began, and then tried again, "Debbie, I . . ."

"Rob? what's the matter with you?" She asked, her voice curious and crisp and normal. I felt like fifty kinds of baboon.

"Will you go sailing with me this Saturday?" I blurted.

"Really? On the *Dragonfly?*" She sounded so excited that my confused brain sort of went back together, and I could talk without sounding like such a fool. We made plans on the phone, deciding that she'd bring the lunch and I would get chilled Cokes, and that we'd probably start early in the morning, say maybe eight o'clock.

When I told Doyle, he said in his dry way, "That's why they call boats like the *Dragonfly* the 'day sailer,' boy. You'd best take some suntan lotion. The sun can get wicked on the water." He paused. "And, Rob . . ."

"What?" I was afraid he'd change his mind.

"Nothing," he said, clamping his jaws tight. "Just be

careful. Summer weather's unpredictable, and neither you nor Deb have all that much sailing experience."

"I hear you," I said, but I wasn't really thinking too much about what Doyle was saying. In my head I was already sailing out there in the blue bay with Debbie, and I was watching the wind whip her dark hair around her face.

The week meandered by real slowly, and on Friday I didn't think the hours would ever pass at all. As for the night, I couldn't sleep. I lay turning and thumping my pillow and got up a hundred times to look at the sky from the bedroom window. Doyle was on night shift, so there was only Elmer to wonder why I was up at 3:00 A.M. heating myself some milk, or why I walked out into the frog-busy night to make sure that the extra lifejacket I was bringing was in good condition. There were stars in the night sky, big, white guys with such brilliance that they looked like glass marbles. "You keep fair," I whispered, eyes turned to the sky. "Make sure you give us fine weather tomorrow, hear me?"

And still I couldn't sleep. Elmer whuffed and snored at the foot of my bed. I stared at the sweep of sky outside the window as it turned from black to cobalt and then to gray. I finally dozed off, and then it seemed minutes until Doyle was letting himself into the house.

He made flapjacks and bacon, and we had breakfast together, Doyle carefully going over the rules. "I want you to be careful," he said at least fifty times.

"Kurt, I know all that stuff."

He rolled his eyes. "I've raised a child genius. Look, you! The sea is no joke, I've told you this often, but I'm telling you again. Keep an eye on those clouds. You don't want to be caught out in a storm."

I was impatient, but I knew I couldn't stop Doyle once he started going, so I nodded. When he started telling me about a time he got caught in a storm, though, it was too much. "Kurt, look. I'm not going to get caught in any storm. I won't do anything dumb. Honest!"

He glared at me. "Guess I sound like a mother hen," he sighed. "I just want you two to be safe, son."

He'd called me "son" before, but somehow today it made me look at old Doyle more carefully. Had Pa ever called me that? Had he ever wondered or worried about my being safe? Softly, nibbling against my mind, came Pa's voice: *Stupid little dummy, who told you to stay out of the house while I was out? Little creep, you ate all the food I had! I'm going to make you pay for that, jerk!*

I closed my eyes and the darkness of that loneliness, the ache of it, slid near. No, I told myself, push it back. Push it back and don't think of it today. Go away, Pa. Can't you let me be happy?

Doyle was looking at my bottles of Coke, shaking his head. "You sure you have enough?" he demanded. "Looks to me you're going to feed an army with this. Or are you going away for six weeks, I wonder?"

Go away, Pa, I thought, silently. There's no room for you here. I closed the door on my loneliness and the ache and turned to Doyle. "You should see what Debbie's bringing." I grinned. "Chicken and salad and sandwiches . . ."

"Likely you'll eat the whole thing," he shot back.

"You're a bottomless pit." But he smiled, and there was no sting to the words. "Got to get a raise to afford your grocery bills," he added.

"I'm worth it," I said.

We grinned at each other. It was weird. Doyle could tell me how worthless I was, and it wouldn't bother me. I could tell him he was all wet, and he'd laugh.

"Well, if you're ready I'll drive you down to the marina before I hit the sack," Doyle said.

I ran to my room and combed my hair. Don't ask me why. The wind would just ruffle it right back up, but I did, anyway. In the mirror, my face looked back at me, no longer starved and scared, but fuller, the brown eyes excited. I moved back, arching my muscles and seeing my chest fill with new weight. Doyle stuck his head through the door. "You going to admire yourself all day?"

A thought suddenly came to me. I frowned. "I eat a lot, don't I?" He looked at me, surprised. "I mean, it must cost a lot. Guards don't make a lot of money, You've said so."

He made a sound like "Tchah." "We make out okay," he said. "You don't have to worry about that." I started to ask another question, but he stopped me with a weather report. "Says we'll get a shower or so this afternoon. Mackerel sky means changeable weather, so be careful."

He drove me to the marina. It was close to eight, and the blue bay was about as sparkling as the sky. I started to get the *Dragonfly* ready and was nearly done when I heard the car engine. In a little while, Debbie came down the steps of the seawall. Behind her, carrying a picnic basket, was Aaron Carmody.

For a horrible moment I thought he was coming along too, but he'd only arrived to give more advice. He was one of those adults who felt he had to explain everything to kids three times in case they were thick or hard of hearing. He started out by saying he trusted Doyle's judgment, then proved he didn't.

"If Kurt believes you're ready to sail, then you are," he said, real pompously. "I just want you to realize that the bay can be very changeable. That means that the weather can switch from calm to stormy at a moment's notice. You have to watch the sky at all times. That means, be alert."

Debbie was ready to die. "Oh, Dad . . ."

He went on and on. "I'd like you to stay close to the shore. That means I don't want you to sail beyond the bottleneck. Do you understand?" he asked, hopefully. I said, yes, I did. "The sea is a very difficult thing to predict. That means . . ."

He went on like this for ten minutes. I timed him. Finally Debbie reminded him that it was getting to be opening time at the hardware store. I couldn't resist. "that means you'd better hurry downtown right away," I said, and he gave me a dirty look.

When he left, Debbie and I looked at each other and started to laugh. We began loading her food on the *Dragonfly,* and she said, "I was really worried about the weather. Mom nearly didn't let me go because she said it might rain." She made a face. "Parents!"

I said, "Yeah," then realized I was thinking of Doyle.

I also thought, for the first time in a long while, about my own mom, and how I could hardly remember anything about her except that she held me in her lap when I was little and read stories to me and taught me my letters. Funny, but standing on the quay with Debbie I remembered that Mom's arms had been warm, her smile sweet. I couldn't remember her face, but I could see her smile.

Debbie was watching, sensing my mood, so I said, "We'd better get out of here before your dad figures he needs to give us some more instructions."

Debbie knew her way around boats, so we didn't take long to sail out into the bay. The air was warm and the sun was hot on my back. In the tangy, powerful, salt-and-wind air, Debbie and I chattered about nothing much. We shifted sail and ran free for a while till the shore seemed far away.

For the first couple of hours it was terrific. We had the bay to ourselves. Soon, though, other boats came onto the water. We ignored them, floating along, idly talking, sunning, running free, and then stopping to sun some more. After a while the sun got so hot that we both dived off into the water and swam a bit. The air was warm, but the water was cold, and we soon climbed back onto the *Dragonfly* and lay on our backs, sunbathing. I teased Debbie about being afraid of sharks. She said that there weren't any sharks in the bay that she knew of.

That made me remember a story Pa had once told me when he was working the boats. He'd talked about pulling in a seven-foot shark one time. "It had a baby shark inside it," I told Debbie. "The baby shark had swallowed another fish. And inside the third fish was a kid's rubber ball. It was all cruddy and everything, but Pa said he could still see the ball'd been a red one."

She said, "Ugh, I bet you and your father had plenty of adventures together. Do you miss him?"

Did I miss him? I could have laughed! "I dream about him," I said, which was the truth.

"Bet you're waiting for him to come and get you like he promised," Debbie went on. She sat up in the boat, threw back her dark hair. I remembered the lie I'd told her a long time ago, and it made me feel uncomfortable.

All of a sudden, she touched my arm. "Rob, over there!" I looked. A Sunfish was coming toward us. On board were Dan and Seth, and their pal Jason! "They see us," she groaned. "They'll ruin everything!"

I knew that if they caught up to us they'd do just that. I knew. They'd hang around and try and capsize us and make comments . . . My face started to burn with anger. No way! I thought. I won't let them mess today up! I glanced back at the gaining Sunfish, and then out over my shoulder. The dark teeth of the bottleneck were very near. The buoys that marked it bobbed in the water.

"Watch out," I told Debbie. "I'm coming about."

"Where are you going?" Debbie asked. Suddenly, she saw the dark rocks coming up on us. "Rob, you can't! My dad would kill me!"

I didn't think of what Doyle would do to me. "They'll ruin the whole day for us," I said through gritted teeth. "You want that?" She shook her head and looked doubtfully at the rocks. "They won't follow us beyond that on their Sunfish," I added.

The wind was pushing us along, and the *Dragonfly* actually seemed to fly as we skimmed over the water toward the dark rocks. I felt a heady power, a feeling that nothing and no one in the whole world could hurt or stop me. I knew that I could do anything I wanted, anything!

"They're still following us," Debbie groaned.

"Let them!" I had the feeling I wasn't Rob Holland any more; I was a fearless captain in some old story. The rocks came closer. So what? What were some old rocks to me? I concentrated hard on sailing the *Dragonfly* through the narrow waters of the bottleneck.

Debbie gave one gasp as we maneuvered past a huge rock that towered over us. Then, another. The water of the bottleneck flowed swiftly, churned white by the narrowness of the passage and the rocks above and below the water. I saw barnacles clinging to the rocks, heard the slosh of seawater against them. Debbie cried out as we nearly hit a submerged rock. "Oh, Rob . . ." she gasped, and then we were out of the bay and into the ocean!

I maneuvered the *Dragonfly* past one last clump of rocks. They were shaped like a big dark hand, the knuckles above the water, the thumb pointing up toward the sky, the fingers hidden and slimy under the waves. Even now, as high as I was and as good as I felt, that rocky hand gave me a chill, a check. I glanced over my shoulder at the white water rushing through the bottleneck. I'd made it! The Sunfish was far behind.

"They gave up," Debbie said. Her eyes were wide with surprise and admiration. "Rob, you really did it! I didn't think you could. Even Dad doesn't manage the bottleneck that easily."

Suddenly, I was starving! Debbie got out the lunch basket, I opened the Cokes, and we spread all the food out on the bottom of the softly rocking boat. Letting down our sail, we lolled out there in the wide sea and ate. The sandwiches and chicken were the best things I'd ever eaten. "It's the sea air," Debbie said. Doyle should have seen Deb. She ate a lot, too!

"Out here is different from the bay. You can feel it," Debbie said after a little while. It was true. Back in the bay, you felt somehow hemmed in, coddled in a safe place. Out here there was no shoreline and no horizon. The Atlantic stretched right into the sky. It gave me a sense of freedom, and I wanted to stand right up in the boat and flex my muscles and give a war whoop.

Debbie was smiling at me. "You're different out here, too," she said. I asked her what she meant. "I don't know." She closed her green eyes against the sun, then opened them and looked at me in a way that made my heart do flip-flops against my ribs. "You're just not the same." Suddenly, she grinned. "You know, once he's meek, mild-mannered Clark Kent. Next minute, is it a bird? Is it a plane? No, it's SuperRob!"

"Get out of here!" But she was right, I thought, smugly. I'd shown those creeps what I could do! I felt too good to be sitting in the boat. "I'm going swimming," I told her.

"Right after eating? Rob, you are crazy. You'll get cramps in that cold water." She snuggled herself down into the bottom of the boat, closed her eyes. "I'm napping."

Her face was upturned to the sun, her sweet face with the scattering of freckles. I wanted to bend down and kiss her, but I didn't have the nerve. Maybe Super-Rob wasn't all that brave, I thought.

I sat close to her, one arm thrown over the side of the *Dragonfly,* one arm touching hers. There was a silky feel to her skin, and I ran my finger down her arm. She reached out and caught my hand, held it lazily.

"If you close your eyes," she said drowsily, "you can see colors through your eyelids."

I tried it. The sun made shimmery colors behind my closed lids. I opened my eyes again and checked everything out. The boat sat easy with sails down. The bottleneck with its marker buoys was far away. The water looked calm.

I yawned. Everything looked good; everything was calm. I'd close my eyes for just a second. For just a second, I told myself, drifting away. Then I'd wake up and watch Debbie as she slept . . .

"Rob! Wake up!"

I came awake quickly, swimming to the surface of things as if I'd been underwater. I felt groggy, disoriented—and I couldn't see. I blinked my eyes really hard. I still couldn't see.

"Rob, it's fog!" came Debbie's voice next to me. "It must've started up while we were sleeping."

Debbie was scared. How? was all I could think. We had gone to sleep in sunshine. Now, all of a sudden, there was no sun at all. Everything around us was gray, as if somebody had poured smoke all over the water. The smoky gray mist was wet to touch, but it wasn't really rain.

"How?" I said out loud.

"It must've started to rain while we were sleeping, and the rain was warmer than the sea. That's what made the fog." Debbie was struggling to keep her voice steady. "It happens a lot out here, but usually there's warning. What are we going to do, Rob?"

"We've got to get back," I said. Debbie looked at me, face pale in the dense gray mist.

"How are we going to do that? I can't even *see* the bottleneck," she whispered. She looked ready to cry.

Far off in the distance, I saw a sudden flash of light, followed by a ringing sound. "What's that?"

Debbie's eyes widened, and I saw the relief in them. "I'm so dumb!" she cried. "I forgot—the buoys by the bottleneck! In foggy weather they send out a light and that bell rings every few minutes to keep boats off the rocks."

"So all we have to do is head toward the light and sound," I said, like there was nothing to it. I didn't add, and we'll get through the bottleneck somehow, too.

We got the sails rigged, and I waited for them to puff with wind. Nothing. Everything was still, except for the bell ringing from the buoy. The whole world seemed asleep under the layer of gray mist.

"We're not moving," Debbie whispered. "Oh, I wish we hadn't been so dumb! Falling asleep in the middle of the ocean . . ."

"Forget that," I said. Inside, I was mad at myself for getting us into this. I snapped, "Grab an oar and row toward that light."

We pulled out the oars and started to row. The compass, tied to the mast, told us we were heading northwest. The flash of light that came from the buoy looked like far-off sheet lightning, but the bell was getting nearer. I strained my eyes, trying to pick out that huge rock, the one that looked like a hand.

"Can you see it?" Debbie whispered. She was staring, too.

"No, nothing. That sound's awful close, though, Debbie. I . . ."

"There!" Debbie shrieked suddenly. I nearly lost my oar. She pointed. I saw it, looming out of the gray like a huge dead hand ready to grab us! Debbie was still screaming, but when I leaned on my oar, she did too. I heard the scrape of the *Dragonfly*'s hull against the rock. Another minute and it would have crushed us!

Debbie was making little sounds, like crying. I was shaking hard. "It's a good thing you saw it, Debbie. We . . . we know where it is now. We'll try and sail around it." I looked at her, pleading. "We'll be okay."

For a second, she was quiet. Then she said, "Yeah, we'll be okay." I heard the bravery in her voice. I really loved that girl, especially when she said "Okay, Super-Rob. What now? Shall we try it again?"

We did try. Carefully, carefully, inching our way through the gray water and gray air, we tried to sneak by the big rock. We watched for it like hawks, poking our oars out every few seconds to make sure there were no rocks on either side. Suddenly, I felt something strange happening to the *Dragonfly.* Debbie felt it, too.

"Rob, we're *moving,*" she cried.

I glanced at the sails. They hung limp and dead like a bat's folded wings. But then how . . . We were moving, all right, moving away from the huge rock, away from the bottleneck! "What is it?" I asked. At the same time I knew. "The current." I groaned.

We were caught in a riptide and it was pushing us out to sea! The flash of light that guarded the bottleneck was growing farther and farther away.

"Row!" I shouted at Debbie. "It'll take us right out to sea!"

We struggled to pull out of the riptide, but it wouldn't let us go. It *wanted* us out at sea! The fog was so thick now, I couldn't even see Debbie's expression as she leaned down on her oar, hair falling to cover her face.

"No use, Rob! It's got us. It'll take us out, and we'll never make it back to land." Her voice was thick with tears. "We'll never get back home."

It was about the way I felt, too, but her misery pulled me together. "We can't give up, Deb. We've got to pull free. Swimmers pull free of riptides, right? We'll just have to ride with it for a while. Then we'll pull free." She shook her head, slowly, but I went on. "Of course we will! And the fog won't last forever."

"Yes, it will. Oh, it will. Once it comes it'll last all night. Listen!" Far off, I heard a deep, mournful sound. "That's a foghorn. The trawlers and cutters are using their foghorns," Debbie moaned.

I was wracking my brain. Doyle had once told me about riptides. You couldn't fight them, but if you went parallel to them, you could free yourself. I shoved my oar into the water. "Debbie, row," I said. "We're going to get out of this!" I tried to put hope into my voice, and maybe she heard it, because she rowed with me. We pulled on those oars so hard we nearly broke our backs, we rowed and rowed some more. And when it seemed like we'd never make it, the *Dragonfly* began to move, very slightly.

"Is she breaking free?" Debbie puffed.

"No. Look!" The sails were slowly filling with air. There wasn't much breeze, but there was just enough! I threw my oar into the boat and scrambled for the tiller. "We'll get out of this yet, Deb."

We cheered as the *Dragonfly* began to move. Where were we heading? Nobody cared! All we wanted to do was to leave the riptide behind us. We could tell when it had let go of us. Both Debbie and I let out loud whoops. "Ee-yayyy!" Debbie shouted. "Mark one for old SuperRob!"

"And for Debbie, Wonder Woman of Laysner!" I yelled.

I'd have said more, except right then there was another sound. It was a sound I'd never heard before, and it went off right behind us. I turned, dazed, and saw something huge and dark plowing toward us out of the mist.

"Rob!" Debbie shrieked. "A ship! It's a ship! It's going to hit us, Rob!"

I pulled hard on the tiller, pulled hard for our lives, but it wasn't hard enough. The wake of the vessel caught the *Dragonfly,* pushing her onto her side. As she capsized, a huge yellow light glinted on the fog and the water. The throb of engines moved away from us. I was hitting the cold water, sinking under it.

I surfaced, yelling, "Debbie!" I didn't hear her answer. I yelled again. "Deb! Where are you?"

"Here!" She was clinging to the side of the *Dragonfly.*

"Are you okay?" I asked, as I swam up to the boat. She nodded. "We've got to right her," I said. "I'll climb on the centerboard."

"Why?" she asked me. "We'll die anyway. We don't know where we are. We'll just drift, and if a ship doesn't chop us in two, we'll just drown or be caught by another rip."

"Don't talk like that!" I snapped at her. Then I was sorry. This mess was all my fault. "Debbie, I'm sorry . . ."

My words were cut short by that awful sound again. I jerked my head up and saw the pale, dusty light of the ship's lights trying to pierce through the fog. "They're coming back this way!" Debbie gasped. "They saw us and they're coming back!"

As if to answer her, a voice sang out of the darkness.

"Ahoy, out there! We see you. We're coming to pick you up. Ahoy, out there!"

Debbie let out a squeal of joy. I thought, What's Doyle going to say?

CHAPTER 10

I was in plenty of trouble. When the trawler that had fished us out of the water took us in, Mr. Carmody and Doyle were waiting for us. Mr. Carmody told me right out that he wished I'd drowned out there. I deserved it, he said, for putting his daughter in danger. Debbie was forbidden to phone me, see me, talk to me in school. He grounded her for a hundred years. Then he marched her home, leaving me with Doyle.

Doyle didn't say a word as we saw to the *Dragonfly,* which had been towed in by the trawler. He let me strip the sails and moor her, wipe her down. Then, when we were in the van going home, he let me have it.

He wasn't mad at me—shouting or hitting mad, that is. I could have stood that. He was cold and silent mad, bitter and shut in the way he'd been in the old days.

"What you did was stupid and totally unnecessary," he said. "If those boys were annoying you as you say, all you had to do was to come ashore and wait till they'd gotten tired of their foolish game. You know it; I know it. But you had to show off. Do you know how worried we've been? We alerted the coast guard, sent for help in finding you . . ."

He bit off every word as if he personally hated its guts. You could see he hated mine. And could I blame him? He'd taken me in, trusted me, lent me that precious boat of his.

"I wasn't showing off," I muttered.

"Weren't you?" Colder than the north wind. "I'd hopes for you," he began, then he stopped and looked at me with those cold eyes. "Get out of my sight," he growled.

I hated him and I hurt. I told myself that it hadn't been my fault, but nobody else felt that way. Mr. Fitz told me as much next day in school.

"A sailor always watches the weather, and he never falls asleep on the job," Mr. Fitz lectured, "especially not in the Atlantic!"

He made it plain he thought I'd been stupid. So did the other kids in school, especially Debbie's friends. The only ones who didn't act like I was some kind of lowlife were Seth and Dan. That was a surprise. I'd figured those two would jump on the bandwagon right away; instead, they were nice about it. They sat next to me in RC32 and didn't make fun or try to get me in trouble. At the cafeteria during lunch, they sat with me and we talked. I found out that Seth's father whaled on him a lot, like Pa. Dan told me *his* folks were never around much and didn't care what he did when they were.

They wanted to know about Doyle. "How come he's got a nice house and a boat on a guard's salary?" Seth wanted to know. I said, his pension. "Get real!"

Seth snorted. "He's a cop—was one, anyway. Cops don't get rich on their pensions." He sniggered suddenly. "He was one hard-nosed cop, Jason says. Did you know that Doyle's daughter, Alma, used to be good friends with Jason?"

"No way," I said. But then I remembered how Doyle had talked about Jason and things started to make sense.

"The old man hated the idea," Dan added. "I heard he pushed Alma around so much that she took off. You know," he added, "you shouldn't let him push you around, Rob."

They both looked at me, but I just shrugged. As bad as my life with Doyle had become, I couldn't bad-mouth him. Not then. That would come later.

It happened about a couple of weeks after the incident of the fog. Doyle treated me, most times, like I wasn't there, and I responded the same way. If I had had any place to go, I'd have gone, and maybe he wished I'd do just that. One afternoon after school he came down on me real hard.

"I'm hearing stuff I don't want to," he started off. "I hear you're running with the wrong crowd at school. Seth Boudine and that sidekick of his, Dan, are your pals—that's what I'm hearing."

I stared at him, hating him. He was dressed for his night shift at the warehouse. He had on his guard's suit and his guard's hat, and his weapon was packed at his side. He looked like a cop and sounded like one, and I remembered what Dan had said about not letting Doyle push me around. "Your hearing's real good," I said.

The frown over his eyes tightened and so did his

thin lips. "You're getting to have a fresh mouth," he snapped.

"What the hell do you care about my mouth—or about my friends?"

He raised his hand like he was going to hit me. Go ahead, I thought, hit me! If he touched me, I was walking out of there. But at the same time, I was starting to shake in the old way, shake so hard that my shoulder bones nearly jangled my ribs. He stared at me for a second, then dropped his hand. "Your marks are slipping," he accused.

I hated the grit of tears in my eyes. "What do you care? I'm nothing to you."

He started breathing hard. He sounded like Elmer, who was whining beside him, not liking the vibes he was picking up from us. "Tough guy, right? You think you know it all. Know what you are? Just a punk kid. That's all, just a punk kid! You don't know anything about life.

I was just as mad as he was. "So, I'll leave!" I shouted at him. "I'll leave, okay? Let me get my stuff together . . ." I stopped suddenly, realizing I had nothing. Whatever I had, he had given me. That made me even angrier. "You just watch me!" I yelled at him.

"Fine. That's the way you feel—take a hike. Go wherever you want to." He turned his back to me, starting stamping toward the door, stopped there, and whirled to throw one last glare at me and a handful of words. "You make me sick!"

Then he was gone. "You make me sick, too!" I shrieked at the closed door. I was shaking so hard the words came out tangled. I wished that the van would blow up as he started it and tore down the road, as if he wanted to pop all the tires. I felt like kicking him, so I kicked the door instead. I kicked it again. Elmer started to growl and bark.

"Oh, shut up you stupid dumb dog!" I yelled. Elmer growled again. I picked up a magazine and threw it at him. I didn't mean to hit him, but it caught him in his broad beam. He yelped and dived down under the couch. Then he started to growl, but it sounded more like crying. I felt sick to my stomach and mean. Meaner than dirt.

I got down on my hands and knees and poked my face down till it was eye level with Elmer. I pleaded with him to come out. He eyed me suspiciously. "I'm not mad at you," I told him. "I'm mad at Kurt." He whined. "Oh, El, please come out!"

But he didn't, he just hunkered there and whined at me. Into my mind poured a memory of Pa kicking a dog back someplace down the road, a small, scroungy, lost and hungry hound who had come to us hoping for some handouts and a little love. Tears started in my eyes and I bit my lip to hold back the crying, but I couldn't shut away Pa's voice. *Yes, Robby. You're acting more like my son now; you really are. Hurting Elmer makes you more like me.*

"Stay there if you want to," I told Elmer. "Stay there and do whatever you want to!" He whined again, and it made my eyes burn with unshed tears. I couldn't stand being there a second more. I jumped up and ran to the door, hauling it open so hard I thought it'd fall off the hinges. I slammed it shut and ran out into the twilight.

It was just turning dark. Long fingers of dark sky were stretching out from a lilac horizon. I started to walk toward the town, meaning to walk and walk and walk along the seawall. Who does he think I am? I said to myself. I pull my weight. I help clean, I cook, I work for my keep. Where does he get off? He doesn't own me. I do what I like!

I was walking so fast that I found myself in town before I knew what happened. It was a nice evening, so plenty of kids were out, some of them hanging around Carmody's. I wondered where Debbie was, and that made another knot inside my already knotted gut. I was starting to turn off to the road by the seawall when I heard Seth Boudine call my name. "Hey, Rob!" Seth shouted.

I turned uncertainly and saw him and Dan coming toward me. I hesitated, then walked toward them. "What's happening?" Dan asked.

I shrugged. "Not much. I was going for a walk."

Dan snickered and glanced at Seth, who said, "So were we."

Seth grinned. "Yeah, so why not stick with us, Rob? It'll be more fun than a walk with that fat old dog of Doyle's." He put a hand on my shoulder. "Come with us."

"Where?" I asked. He tightened his grip on my shoulder and I remembered a time when Doyle had touched me on the shoulder like this and told me he was proud of me. Now he couldn't stand my guts! "Where're we going?"

"Thought we'd make it down to the marina," Dan said, squinting up into my face. He winked. "Have a little fun."

I figured, what the heck. It wasn't too long a walk to the marina and tonight even the company of Seth and Dan seemed good. We walked through the town and onto the road that hugged the seawall. There, Dan slid a pudgy hand into his pocket, pulled out something, and snapped a lighter. He slid the something into his mouth and pulled in air. A sicky-sweet smell competed with the sea wind.

"Have a puff?" he asked, passing the joint to me. I shook my head. "Doyle's good little boy," Dan jeered. "He's not here to see you now!"

That made me grab the joint and stick it between my lips. It felt moist from Dan's lips, and that in itself made me feel sick. Worse was the rush of smoke into my lungs. I gasped and coughed while the guys laughed.

"Nothing like a bone to clear the fumes in your head," Seth said when I'd quit my hacking. "You look uptight tonight, Rob. Have another drag."

This time, it didn't sear my lungs as bad, but I didn't like the taste. My head whirled from it, probably because I'd coughed so hard. "Nothing to it," I told Seth, and he punched me in the shoulder.

"Now you're talking."

We walked along, puffing and talking. I was feeling very little pain. My problems with Doyle seemed far away. My eyes felt a bit hazy, and I had to blink several times to see what Seth was pointing to.

"That's the marina." I laughed. "We got here. Whoopee!"

"Shut up, will ya?" Seth said. He started laughing himself, though, and staggered as he climbed the side of the seawall and wobbled down the stone steps. Dan followed. It took me longer. I knew I was walking, but my feet didn't, and somehow I couldn't stand too well. I finally had to scoot down on my bum. I was giggling as I joined Dan and Seth on the sandy beach.

They were throwing stones into the ocean. "Don't do that," I giggled. "You might hit one of those boats."

"Shut up, Rob," Dan said and handed me the joint again. "Take this and shut up."

I dragged on the joint again, watching dreamily as Seth and Dan threw more stones. The stones seemed to whirl slow motion through the air, splashing down in water that was bright with shimmery color. The dark boats were shadows against the sand and moonlight and looked huge.

"Rob's smoked this one out. What else you got?" Seth asked Dan, who dug around in his tight jeans. After a while he came out with a small packet of white powder. Seth grinned. "That's *nice,* man."

I watched groggily as Dan pulled out a piece of glass and shook some of the white powder onto it. He produced a straw. "Have a snort, Rob," he invited. "Jason's stuff is excellent."

"Jason gave you the coke?" I said, but my tongue

wouldn't curl around the words. What came out was, "Jasonuvucoke?"

"Hey, he's learning another language. He's a graduate from the Dummy Room," Dan crowed. He inserted the straw into his nostril, pinched the other shut, and breathed white powder in. He looked so funny doing it that I couldn't stop laughing. I flopped backward and felt the cool powder of sand under me. Like snow, only not so cold.

"Whoo-pee!" I howled.

Seth took his turn snorting up the coke. Then he stood swaying, looking toward the marina. "Know what we should do?" he asked. "We should take some stuff off the boats. We could sell it."

"Yeah," Dan said, and he started giggling. "Can you see old man Carmody's face? He'll come down here for a sail and he'll go, 'My tiller's not here!' "

We all howled. It was a big joke. "Let's do it," I tried to say, but only gobbledygook came out of my mouth.

Seth started walking toward the boat. Dan weaved after him. I watched for a while, as they tried to board one of the boats. The sight of those two trying to get onto a boat was hilarious, and I laughed till my sides hurt. Then I saw that Seth had managed to crawl into one of the boats and was throwing stuff—lifejackets, it looked like—out to Dan.

It seemed like too much fun to miss. I got to my knees, but that was as far as I could go. I started to crawl over the sand toward the guys. "Wait for me!" I tried to shout in my new, mixed-up language.

"We can sell it. We can sell it," Dan was chanting.

"Jason knows where to sell everything. We'll make a big score, man. Hey, here's Rob. Seth, let him do Doyle's boat, huh? Let him do the *Dragonfly.*"

"Go get it man," Seth agreed. "Sic Doyle's boat."

I made growling dog noises as I crawled down the long quay toward the bobbing *Dragonfly.* Then I grabbed the prow of the boat and managed to haul myself on board. "Do it!" Dan urged.

Do what? I wondered. I got to my feet, collapsed. "He's out of it," Seth slurred. "We'll do her." He and Dan lurched down the quay and started reaching to get into the *Dragonfly.* "Let's really smash her up good," Seth told Dan. "Jason'd like that—us smashing Doyle's boat good."

Suddenly, down in the depths of my foggy, groggy brain, it hit me that they wanted to hurt the boat. They wanted me to smash her mast, tear up her centerboard, ruin the *Dragonfly.*

"No," I tried to say. "Don't!"

"He ain't making sense," Dan said. He started to come aboard. I grabbed his foot and pushed, and he fell back into the water with a splash. Seth managed to get into the boat, and he grabbed my hair and punched me in the face.

"You crazy?" he shouted.

Punch, punch. I was dizzier than I'd been before. I held onto Seth around the waist, trying to keep him from doing anything to the boat. Dan had hauled himself onto the quay and was standing there weaving and dripping and cursing me. "You. When I get you—"

Suddenly a big voice began to boom down at us,

and a spotlight went on. "What's happening down there?" the voice shouted.

Seth pushed me down and jumped for the quay. He made it and sprinted on shaky legs for the beach. Dan followed. I wanted to run, too, but I couldn't move.

Something weird was happening in my head. It was like the *Dragonfly* was closing in, like an accordion that wanted to squeeze the life out of me. "There's another one on the boat!" I heard a big voice boom, and it sounded louder than thunder.

It had to be a nightmare! I felt the thunder breaking all around me. My heart was pounding, and the world was closing in. I felt a kind of tingling numbness together with the tightness and the pounding, and there was this head that seemed to hang upside down over me. "He's on some kind of drug trip, a bad one!" I heard the big voice boom. "Call the police!"

Light and darkness swirled around me and I could hear Pa, not in my head where he usually was, but outside, shouting that he was going to beat me to a pulp this time. "Why were you trying to vandalize the boats?" Pa was bellowing.

There was more darkness and noise, and flaring blue lights. Pa wanted me to go with him somewhere. I didn't want to go, but Pa picked me up and carried me into the darkness, and I cried and begged and sobbed. Then there were more voices, and the world seemed to go blooie around me and things got quiet all of a sudden. And I heard a familiar voice say, "He's had something. God knows what. I think he's coming out of it, though."

My head ached, I realized, and my eyes ached too,

when I opened them and saw Doyle's face hanging over mine. I tried to ask him what was happening, but I couldn't find the words, and anyway, he told me.

"You're flying, Robby," he said. I felt an arm around my shoulders, supporting me. "It's all right."

I felt thankful for a minute, and then Pa was back again, Pa murderous and menacing. "I'm sorry, Pa," I whimpered. He didn't move. "I didn't know what they were going to do. I didn't."

You jerk! You creep! You scum! I know why you did it. You wanted to get even with Kurt Doyle, wanted to hurt him. I'm going to give you what you deserve, you dirty little hypocrite.

"I'm sorry," I wailed, and I tried to curl up into a ball to protect my face and stomach as best I could. "I'll be good, Pa. I promise. I won't be bad any more, I swear . . ."

You can't be good, you! Pa's voice seemed to bellow. *Take your punishment like a man.*

I whimpered. From far away I heard Doyle's voice. "I'm going to take you home and put you to bed. Seth and Dan swear that all you've had is grass, though laced with God alone knows what. It's wearing off, whatever you had. You've been on a bad trip is all."

It was Doyle, not Pa. How had he gotten here? But now that he was here, maybe he could calm Pa down and stop him from punishing me.

"Rob," Doyle said from far off, "you listen to me. You're a good boy, and don't you believe any different. You put up a fight to keep them from ruining the *Dragonfly.* Even spaced out of your mind, you couldn't do anything wrong." Pa's bloodshot eyes and furious voice faded slowly away as Doyle said, "Don't worry, Rob, I've got you."

Peace, quietness—it was like I was on the boat with Doyle, with the wind flapping the sails and the waves washing against the hull of the *Dragonfly.* My eyelids felt heavy and my body felt like it weighed a hundred pounds. I would have fallen, but Doyle was holding me up.

"You're going to be all right." Doyle's voice was sliding away into the distance. And then I thought he said, "I lost one already, and I'm not going to lose you too. Don't worry, Rob. I've got you."

CHAPTER 11

"Hey, Rob," Mr. Fosse called to me as I was heading through the parking lot with my bag of Kentucky Fried Chicken. "Going to take Kurt his dinner?"

"Yeah, Mr. Fosse. Is it okay if I eat with him?"

Mr. Fosse came over to me. He was ready to leave for the night, and he had his light jacket slung over one arm. When he came nearer, I saw he looked worried.

"Rob," he said, "do you know, offhand, whether Kurt has anything on his mind?"

"I don't think so," I said. "Why?"

"Nothing I can put my finger on. He seems like his mind is a million miles away sometimes." Mr. Fosse tried to make a joke. "I figured maybe you were working him too hard."

I laughed politely, but Mr. Fosse's words worried me. Come to think of it, Doyle had seemed thoughtful lately, a lot more thoughtful than usual. Mr. Fosse play-punched my shoulder. "You're probably what the doctor ordered, Rob, you and that dinner. Take care, huh?"

I said goodnight to Mr. Fosse and walked past the

high, steel-link fence to the tall locked gate. "Hey, there!" I yelled. "Chow time!"

Doyle stuck his head out of the little guardhouse a few yards in from the main gate. "What's for dinner?"

He came toward the gate jangling keys, and I looked him over. That last bit Mr. Fosse said about the doctor worried me. How long had it been since Doyle had gone to see a doctor? Could his heart be acting up? I stared at him hard as he opened the door, but I couldn't see anything different about his face.

"Chicken," Doyle was saying. "My favorite. You got plenty of coleslaw this time, did you?" I nodded. "I've got a pot brewing," he went on as we walked toward the guardhouse. "Nice thick black mud, the way I like it."

I cleared my throat. "Maybe you oughtn't drink all that much coffee," I said. "Caffeine isn't good for . . . well, you know, your heart."

He put a heavy arm around my shoulders and massaged my hair with the other hand. I threw a block on him, and he fake-punched me. I slid in an uppercut, which he blocked. "The boy is an expert in medicine already," he said and smiled, but there was a look that glimmered in those sharp blue eyes. Worry? No. More like . . . nerves. What was Doyle nervous about?

We got to the guardhouse and I set out our dinner on the small table there. Usually, he helped me, but today he just stood there, looking out of his guardhouse toward the gate, jangling his ring of keys.

"Kurt," I said, "I saw Mr. Fosse outside." I'd meant

to say he'd been worried about Doyle, but Doyle interrupted me.

"Yeah. A big shipment of electronic games came in to the warehouse today. We're holding them for distribution to the stores." He blinked suddenly, as if he'd been thinking aloud. "What's that about Fosse?"

"He says you're a million miles away when he talks to you," I said. He jangled his keys again. "*Is* something wrong?"

"Forget it," he said lightly and came to sit across the small table from me. "Boss is probably uptight because of the electronic games. They cost a lot, and he's responsible for them."

I nodded. We had an arcade in town with a lot of games. Seth and Dan were always in there playing. I frowned, a piece of chicken half in and half out of my mouth. It was the first time in a long while I'd even thought of Seth Boudine and his sidekick.

The police had taken them into "protective custody" that night when we all went down to the marina. They'd both been higher than kites, and, because Dan had some coke on him, he'd been charged with possession. But Dan and Seth were minors, so nothing happened to them—not even for attempted theft and vandalism.

They'd tried to say it was my idea, but that hadn't washed. I'd been hit pretty hard while trying to save the *Dragonfly,* and, anyway, Doyle was in my corner. He didn't lecture me or yell at me or even give me those cold looks of his. He just stood by me and spoke up for me at the Laysner Police Station, and the cops there believed him.

Later, he'd been mad, but not at me. "Those boys wouldn't say who'd given them the coke or that pot," he'd said, "but I know it was Jason."

"They said it was," I told him, and Doyle had nodded.

"Sure it was. He's clever—too clever to be caught." His eyes had narrowed. "One of these days he's going to slip up, and I'll be waiting."

For a long moment he'd looked past me like I wasn't there. I guessed he was thinking of Alma. Had Jason hurt her in some way? I wished I could ask but didn't dare, and after a while Doyle had turned and put a hand on my shoulder.

"It wasn't only Jason's fault," he'd said. "I was wrong, too. I turned my back on you when you needed help. I was angry when you put yourself and Debbie in danger, but I didn't see beyond my own anger. I didn't realize you hurt, and that was very wrong." He had clipped me gently on the chin. "You don't need to worry I'll let you down again," he had said.

I looked at him now across the table and thought about that time—me, half ready to cry, him serious but smiling, and the warmth of the summer morning golden around us. I knew he had meant every word, and the warmth outside me seemed to rush inside, fill all the dark spaces where the loneliness usually stayed. I believed Kurt Doyle then, really *believed* him, and since that day the old trust had come back. Only, this time, it was better. We were more open with each other. We talked more.

Surely, I thought, if he had a problem, I'd have known about it. I watched him as we ate, watched as he poured us both coffee. His hand was as steady as a rock, but that nervous look was still in his eyes. Also, while we were talking he'd suddenly go silent, just stop, as if his thoughts were miles away. He came right back, though, when I told him how Mr. Lind, my English teacher, had read my paper on Kipling's poems to the class.

Doyle opened his eyes real wide. "You mean, it was that bad?"

I pretended to throw a drumstick at him. "No! It was that good!"

He pretended to frown. "He must've made some mistake," he said. "Tell me what you wrote."

I'd brought the paper with me, but suddenly felt shy as I pushed it across the table. There was a big A on top, and an "excellent" right underneath. Doyle started to read, tapping the paper with his thick forefinger and glancing back at the A every now and again. I watched him anxiously. When he finished, he looked at me, really serious.

"Did you do this by yourself, Rob? Debbie didn't help?"

I sighed. "She's not supposed to talk to me, remember?" I reminded him. He gave me a don't-give-me-that look, and I nodded. "No, really. I mean, we see each other in school and in RC32, but that's it. There's a lot of creeps who'd tell old man Carmody, otherwise."

He shook his head and tapped the paper again. "This is terrific," he said, all hoarse with pleasure. "This is a really good paper. The language is better than I could come up with." He beamed at me. "You've got a way with words, boy, I'll say that much for you!"

"It wasn't much." I was getting hot listening to him, and yet I wished he wouldn't stop. "I just started writing the paper and it all sort of came out. It wasn't anything."

"It was something, all right," he shot back. "For a kid who didn't know his elbow from an adverb, you're doing fine! Wish Fosse was here. He's always bragging about his kid!" He paused. "You and Debbie should celebrate. She mightn't have helped with this paper, but she did help you a lot in the beginning."

"You know how Mr. Carmody feels." I pushed the chicken away, my appetite suddenly gone. "He won't even let us talk on the phone."

Doyle shoved more coleslaw and chicken on my plate. He plopped on mashed potatoes and drowned them in gravy. "Don't you worry about Aaron. He's a weather vane. As people's opinions about you change, so will his." He pointed a fork at me. "Most people realize you're okay."

Only because of you, I thought. I watched him chow away, and there was a lot I wanted to say. I knew that it was, because Kurt Doyle said it—that everything was working out. Laysner was a small town and they looked up to Doyle. That was why they believed I wasn't so bad.

Like, they saw how Doyle trusted me with the *Dragonfly*. A few days after that marina incident, he'd taken me down to the quay and sailed us both right up to the bottleneck. He taught me to sail through those big, slimy rocks, right through the buoy and the big stone hand. He let me solo, too, and looked proud when I did okay.

"We haven't taken the *Dragonfly* out for a while," I said, breaking the silence that had come on us. "How about tomorrow?"

I expected him to nod, but he wasn't listening. He was staring past my shoulder at something that was making him frown. He twisted and worked his big, square hands in a way that worried me. "Kurt?" I questioned.

He sort of shook himself. "Sure," he said. "We'll take the *Dragonfly* out." He reached for his flashlight and ran his hand on the big clock he kept in the leather pouch at his belt. "I'm going on my rounds now. Can't be too careful."

"Okay." Maybe it was just the shipment of electronic games that was bothering him. "I'll clean up here."

"Good." He hesitated. "You go home and give Elmer an extra run or something. Okay? I've got some walking and checking and thinking to do."

"What about?" I asked.

"Tomorrow," he said, in his old raspy way. He shook his head at me. "Quit looking so dang worried, boy! Everything is under control." He fished in his pants pocket, pulled out a battered wallet. "I need you to do me a favor, though." I nodded. "Stop at the hardware store. I need a hammer and number ten nails."

"You mean—Carmody's Hardware?" He nodded. "Ah, Kurt, this is me, remember? Mr. Carmody would nail me to a wall if I walked in that place."

Doyle said gruffly, "He will not. Business isn't that good that he could turn away a paying customer." He took ten bucks out of his pocket and handed it to me. "Tell him I need it for tomorrow, that I have to have it tonight."

"I don't like it," I said, taking the money. "I have a really bad feeling, Kurt. He'll kill me."

"Go." He grinned.

He left to go on his rounds, and I cleaned up the scraps and walked back to the gate. Doyle met me there, unlocked it, and nodded good-bye, and I walked down the long, empty asphalt road. Something didn't sit quite easy on my mind, and I wasn't happy. I glanced up at the moon—full or waxing gibbous, as Mr. Fitz called it, and wondered if maybe Doyle was acting funny because of the full moon. Mr. Fitz said that the full moon made people act weird sometimes. I fingered the money in my pocket and hoped that the moon wasn't going to affect Mr. Carmody. Then I remembered the last time I'd seen him, mottled with red, angry spots!

I stopped, half-minded to take the ten dollars back to Doyle. But I told myself that, heck, I *was* a paying customer.

I kept telling myself this until I was in town and within a hundred feet of the hardware store. It was still open, but there were only about fifteen minutes to closing time. Hope came to me; I could tell Doyle that the place had been closed. But I thought of the way he had looked at me with pride, and I sighed. I couldn't lie to him. Squaring my shoulders, I walked into the store.

Mr. Carmody I saw right off. He was sitting behind the counter. He didn't look up. "Be right with you," he said.

I walked toward the nails and hammers. I could just grab what I needed, slam the money on the counter, and get out. I could do it fast, zip-zap, and the old man would never know what happened. Now you see Rob Holland, now you don't! But just as I reached for the hammer, the dumb rack slipped and the whole thing fell.

Carmody looked up, and we stared at each other. His face started to get red. My heart started to pump bullets. "The rack slipped . . ." I began, my voice high and nervous. He just stared at me, and I remembered what had happened when Seth and Dan had come in here some time ago. "Kurt Doyle wants a hammer and number ten nails," I went on, desperately. "He sent me."

Mr. Carmody got up and came over toward me. He held his head forward, like a bull charging. "You . . ." he began.

"Hi, Rob." I hadn't seen Debbie before, but there she was behind the counter. She was all flushed, and I realized what she was trying to do. She was trying to help me, trying to make me see that she was my friend, on my side. Her father turned to her.

"Debbie, I told you never to talk to this boy again!" he snapped.

She lifted her head and stared back at him. "Dad," she said, real quiet, "he's my friend."

The way she said that squirted courage into me. Not much, mind you, but enough so that I didn't turn and run out of there. Instead, I listened to old Mr. Carmody snap, "You don't need friends like this."

I cleared my throat. "Mr. Carmody, I imagine I know how you feel about me . . ." He glared at me. "Uh, Mr. Carmody, Kurt really needs the hammer and number ten nails."

He snatched a hammer off the fallen rack, shoved it into my hands. Grabbing a box of nails, he shoved that at me, too. Looking past me, staring at some point behind my ear, he said "That'll be ten seventy-five."

I pulled the ten out of my pocket. That was all I had! "Mr. Carmody, uh, I'm short. I can run home and get the seventy-five cents if you like."

"We're closing," he snapped. "Come get the stuff tomorrow."

"But Kurt needs the things tomorrow." Debbie was watching me, and her green eyes gave me courage. "Mr. Carmody, couldn't I have credit on the seventy-five cents?"

He made a noise like a furious chicken. I looked into that face and suddenly remembered what Doyle had said about Mr. Carmody being a weather vane. "A lot of people would give me credit," I said, slow and clear. "Mr. Fosse at the plant would. My teachers at school would." I drew a long breath and glanced at Debbie, who nodded. Go get him, Rob! "I'm sorry about what happened that day Debbie and I went sailing. I showed pretty bad judgment and nearly got us killed. I was one dumb fool. But just because you don't like me doesn't mean you can't trust me to bring you seventy-five cents tomorrow."

He narrowed his eyes and stared at me like he hadn't seen me before. His lips twitched. It was like he was having a battle inside himself. Finally he said, "I suppose it's all right." He gargled in his throat and added, "You can give the change to Debbie at school tomorrow."

"Yessir," I said. I felt ten feet tall. Behind her father's back, Debbie gave me the victory sign. I watched Mr. Carmody bag the hammer and nails, then handed over the ten. "Thank you," I said, real polite. "See you tomorrow, Debbie."

She smiled and nodded, and her dad didn't say a word. I went out of there walking high on clouds. Once outside, I jumped up in the air and sprinted down the sidewalk like a banshee. When I was out of hearing, I let loose and yipped like an Indian war chief. I'd got Carmody to talk to me! What's more, he'd as much as said it was okay for Debbie and me to be friends again.

He was breaking down. In another few weeks, he'd crumble to the point where he'd let us go out—maybe. And then we would celebrate. I would ask Debbie to go to the movies, maybe . . . or we could walk on the beach.

I was at the crossroads now, and I hesitated. Did I want to go right home? I did not. I suddenly wanted to be by the sea, smell the salt air like I'd done that day Debbie talked to me the first time. I thought of how we'd walked home, watching the gulls wheeling and dipping in the briny air.

I glanced at my watch. It wasn't quite nine-thirty. Elmer would be snoozing on the couch, and he wouldn't mind if I was out for another hour or so. I started to walk toward the long road that wound around the seawall.

At first I walked briskly, and then I jogged for a while. It was bright and warm, and the road ahead gleamed in the moonlight. I felt good about the world, better than I'd ever felt in my life. "Kurt knew," I said to myself, out loud. He'd know that if I just confronted Mr. Carmody, he'd give in. "Kurt knows everything," I said.

He'd known me on that roof. That seemed so long ago, but it wasn't. Barely two seasons separated me, the good-feeling, happy me, from that kid on the rooftop. I thought of that high, windy rooftop and what had driven me there, tried to remember what I'd felt like. I tried to recall the agony and the loneliness and the sadness that was like pain, but the memories wouldn't come tonight. Let the memories stay buried, I told myself.

I walked faster, thinking of Kurt Doyle. I thought that all this time he'd put up with me and put out for me, and I'd never so much as given him a gift. Sure, I'd cleaned the house and cooked a few meals, and I'd sailed with him. But I'd never given him anything. And, come to think of it, I'd never tried to help by pitching in on expenses.

I frowned suddenly. Could Kurt be hurting for money? Was that why he was edgy? Well, if it was, I could get some odd jobs after school. I couldn't hold a steady job till I was sixteen, but until then I could walk dogs or haul trash or rake lawns. And I could really help out . . .

My thoughts broke off and I squinted ahead of me in the moonlit darkness, suddenly aware that I wasn't alone on the road. I didn't realize I'd come this far, but I had to be close to the school. Someone was walking toward me, his outline barely visible. I could hear footsteps, too, clear in the warm moonlight. There was something about those footsteps that jarred my memory—sort of shuffling, tired-sounding footsteps.

I kept on walking briskly, but I kept an eye on the other walker. Now I could see him clearly. He was walking with an odd, forward-thrusting movement, as if his head was the head of a turtle trying to pull free of its shell. His powerful shoulders were slumped forwards.

Prickles ran across my neck. Doyle had told me about Jim Fosse's being nervous of break-ins. Supposing this guy, whoever it was, was some crook? Rob, get it together, I told myself, but the prickly feeling made me turn and start heading back toward town. The other walker spoke.

"Is this the way to Laysner?" he asked.

I stopped. Dead in my tracks, I stopped. The prickling feeling turned to hair-curling fear. I felt a black wave wash through me so fast I nearly fainted. It can't be, I thought. I have to be wrong.

"Man who gave me a lift said that this was the one road into Laysner, but I might have got mixed up. Is this the road to Laysner or isn't it?"

This time, there was no mistaking that impatient, slurred voice. The worst of my nightmares had just come alive.

It was my Pa.

CHAPTER 12

I didn't know what to do. If I stay quiet, I thought, if I don't say a word, he may pass me by and never know. But my breathing was too loud. Maybe my thinking, even, was too loud.

"Well, is this the road to Laysner?" Pa was impatient. I couldn't see him in the moonlight, but I knew what he'd be looking like, all right. I could see the outline of the bristly jowl, heavy with yesterday's beard, the humped nose, the red-speckled eyes above. And why had he come to Laysner, anyway? Probably because somehow he'd found out I was here.

Pa came closer. I knew I should run, but I couldn't. "Sonavagun," Pa said. "It's Rob."

"What are you doing here, Pa?"

"What kind of greeting is that?" There was anger in his voice, but he was holding it down. That small control meant that he was sober, and mean because of it. "Can't you even say hello?"

I gritted my teeth. I'd forgotten how his voice could scare me. "I came looking for you, of course," Pa said.

"I was in New Mexico for a while, but when I come down this way, I heard you was in Laysner."

"How?"

"You're still my son," he said, dangerous-quiet. "Courts can take you away from me, but they still have to tell me where you're at. Heard you had some cushy life here with an old geek at the Cape."

"So?" My heart was pounding against my ribs, and maybe he heard it, because he started laughing.

"You've grown," he said, "but you aren't a man yet." He repeated that. "Not a man yet."

Behind me, I could hear the waves. Wee-sht, wee-sht. Why had I come this way? I asked myself in panic. If I'd gone home to Elmer . . . But that wouldn't have done any good in the long run. Pa would have come looking for me at the house, and he'd have found us easy. Laysner is a small town.

"Robby," he said, and his voice was suddenly soft and wheedling. I knew that voice, all right. Robby, go get me a drink . . . Beg us some money. We don't have any food. Stand on the sidewalk and cry, and somebody'll slip you a buck. "I came just to see you," Pa said. "We're flesh and blood. I haven't eaten and I don't have a job."

"I've got some money at the house. Ten bucks. It's all I have," I said. "I'll give you that and you can go away."

"Old guy don't give you an allowance?" Pa was disgusted. "I could use a place to stay and some grub," he went on. "You just lead the way to the place where you're staying."

"No," I said.

There was a silence. The road, I now realized, was a lonely one. Nobody—walker, bicycle, or car—had come this way since I met up with Pa. The moon slid behind a cloud, and now it was also a dark road.

"I didn't hear you say that." Pa's voice was soft, dangerous. "You take me there, and fast."

I said, "It's Kurt's house, not mine. He has a rule: no one comes into his house unless he asks them."

Pa swore a blue streak. "I'm your father," he snarled. "He better ask me in! I want to rest and get someplace to stay and some money, and I can't see him denying me." He paused, his voice going all coaxing again. "Rob, I haven't taken a drink in a long time. I'm dry."

"I'll bet," I muttered.

"And I'm not going to lay a hand on you. No, sir. Had time to think of that. Blood is thicker than water, and we are blood. I missed you, boy."

There was something in his words that touched a chord in me, made me ache. I wanted to believe Pa, but I knew that the words were the only things that touched me. His voice told me he lied.

"I'm not taking you to Kurt's place without his knowing about it," I said.

He shouted, "You're going against your father!"

"You're not responsible for me. Remember? You signed me away before the Family Court judge," I yelled back. "You said you didn't care whether you ever saw me again. Well, Pa, guess what? I don't care, either. We're even. So turn yourself around and go back to wherever you came from."

There was a bad taste in my mouth, churned up by the way my heart was banging. I felt like throwing up. Was this me, shouting at *Pa?* He couldn't believe it, either, just stood there staring at me.

"Now, listen," he said in a different voice. "I wasn't in my right mind that day in the court. I admit it. I don't mind telling you, either, that we haven't been like father and son. It's a shame and a sadness to me. But you know and I know that this time it will be different."

"Go away, Pa," I whispered.

"Rob, this stranger isn't your pa. I am."

I said nothing, but I thought of all the things that Doyle had done for me.

"He may have been good to you, but remember, boy. No man on earth does good without a motive. Why's he been so good to you, huh?"

"Because he's a kind man!" I shouted.

"No man's plain good. Everybody's got some gimmick, and if you weren't so dumb and stupid you'd know that." The old anger in him was starting to froth out with the words. "No one's so good as to do something only because he's got a good heart . . ."

"You don't know Kurt," I said.

"Huh! He gets paid by the social workers to keep you." Suddenly, he reached and grabbed for my arm. I acted instinctively. Spinning around, I sidestepped him. Pa blinked at me, lunged again.

"You're not going to lay a hand on me again," I told him, tightly. Muscles, fed on Doyle's good food, strong from sailing the *Dragonfly* across the bay and the ocean, snapped at my command. "You're never going to beat up on me again. Now, get out of my life!"

He said, "Never thought I'd see the day when my own son would tell me to go. You may not know it, but when you was little, I starved to feed you after your mother died. Maybe later, I got harsh. Life wasn't easy for me, and I took the drink." He seemed to sigh, and those bowed, powerful shoulders shook. I felt something tighten in my throat, and warned myself. He's just trying to sweet-talk you, Rob. He wants to trick you.

"I just come by to see if you was happy," he said. "I wanted to see for myself. I wanted to meet this man, this Kurt. I still want to. I'll talk to him one time about you, then I'll go away."

Warning signals pinged inside my head. No way, I thought.

"Rob, what harm would it do, meeting your Kurt? Maybe I want to thank him. I'm beholden to him." He drew heavy arms across his chest. "I won't go without seeing Kurt."

The moon was out of the clouds now, and I could see Pa's face. He meant it. He could be stubborn, more stubborn than anyone I knew. He'd hang around Laysner. I thought of him meeting people like Mr. Fosse, Mr. Fitz, and . . . Debbie.

I remembered that lie I'd told Debbie. Pa and Debbie! I winced at the thought. "If you see Kurt, you'll leave?" I demanded.

I saw him nod. "Yeah. I promise, Rob."

When had his promises ever been kept? But I didn't

have much choice. In fact, I had *no* choice. I thought that if I took him to the warehouse now, he'd go. Kurt could give him some money, and Pa would go away.

"I worried about you, Rob," he said, and again that something stupid and hopeful inside me quivered with pain. Maybe he *had* cared, in his own way.

"Okay," I said. "I'll take you to meet Kurt."

Pa said that would be fine with him. He fell into step, glancing across at me. "You're almost as tall as me," he said, and I realized suddenly that tonight was the longest time we'd talked without his cursing or hitting me. "Strong, too."

"That's from sailing," I couldn't help boasting. "I sail a day sailer called the *Dragonfly.* It's our . . . Kurt's boat."

"Well, now. You sail a boat? You used to be all thumbs," Pa chuckled. I gritted my teeth. Dummy, stupid, fumble-fingers.

"Not any more. Kurt taught me to handle that boat real well."

"A little bit of a boat?" Pa prodded. I described the *Dragonfly.* "Those things cost a packet," Pa said. "How does he do that on a retired policeman's salary, huh?"

"He works part-time at the warehouse where we're going," I answered shortly.

We walked quietly for a while. We were almost at the town, when Pa spoke again. "So he works? Foster kids he takes in like a sideline, huh?"

"He didn't take me in for the money! He took me in . . ." I stopped. I didn't want Pa to know about that rooftop. Strange. Earlier on in the evening, I hadn't even been able to remember how I'd felt while standing on the edge of that flat roof. I hadn't been able to recall the feeling of emptiness inside me. Now I could.

Pa chuckled. "Sounds like your Kurt's a smart boy. He's got it made." He lifted a thick hand, rubbed the fingers together. "All the cops I know are on the take," he said, bluntly.

I set my teeth. I didn't want to argue with Pa. I quickened my pace, while he shuffled along beside me, and we cleared through town without anyone seeing us. When we got on that long, lonely stretch to Fosse's warehouse, he started to talk again, telling me about what had happened to him since we'd met at Family Court. I didn't say a word.

Finally, he started to complain. "This warehouse, is it far? My legs are wore out."

"Another couple of miles. If you can't hack it, we can forget it," I said. I hoped he'd give in and go away, but no such luck. He cursed, but kept on walking. His cursing sounded mean. Suddenly, I panicked. What lies was he going to tell Kurt about me?

"Pa . . ." I began, then stopped. In the distance, I could hear police sirens. Pa's head went up, like a hound dog sniffing the air.

"Something's going on," he said. "They're coming this way."

The sirens kept coming nearer. My windpipe suddenly squeezed together as I recalled Kurt's uneasiness earlier this evening, and Mr. Fosse's concern for his shipment. As I was wondering, the whirling blue of a police car's lights started up in the distance, and then whooshed past us into the darkness ahead. What had happened at the warehouse? to Kurt?

I began to run, and Pa puffed behind me. I didn't know what had happened, but I was surely scared for Kurt. I turned the corner and stopped short. There was the Fosse Warehouse gate, wide open, and police cars parked right up close. I picked out Seth and Danny right away. They were standing against two prowl cars, arms wide and legs apart, being searched. I saw Jason, too. He was being read his rights by a big cop.

My heart leaped. They'd caught Jason! Finally, Kurt had gotten him! I wanted to shout with triumph, but I had to find Kurt first. "Where's Kurt?" I asked aloud.

"You tell me, boy." I'd forgotton about Pa, huffing and puffing behind me. "You nearly ran me off my legs. Where's this Kurt, and what's going on?"

I spotted Mr. Fosse. He was standing by the open gate, talking to a couple of cops. But Kurt . . . An awful thought came to me. Was Kurt hurt? I raced forward, ran right up to Mr. Fosse.

"Mr. Fosse, is Kurt all right?" I cried.

The man turned to me like he didn't know me. His face was angry, angrier than I'd ever seen a man look. "What do *you* want?" Mr. Fosse snapped.

I didn't understand. Maybe, I thought, he was all shaken up. It was plain to see what had happened; Seth and Danny and Jason had tried to rob the warehouse and had gotten caught.

"Where is Kurt?" I tried again.

He reached out, grabbed both my shoulders, and started shaking me. "I never want to hear that name again, understand?" He shouted. "You. You were in on this with him! I had a feeling when you came snooping around tonight. You both were laughing behind my back, weren't you?" He shook me again. "I'd have been cleaned out if a police car hadn't come by."

What was he talking about? I started to ask for Kurt a third time, and then I saw him. He was standing with three police officers. They didn't have him spread-eagled against a prowl car, but they were searching him. Searching Kurt? The idea didn't register.

"Your Kurt Doyle left the gate open for those thieves. He was in with them!" Mr. Fosse was saying. "If the police cruiser hadn't come by, they'd have robbed me blind!"

"No!" I shouted. "That's wrong! Kurt hated Jason . . ."

"That was his cover." Mr. Fosse looked weary. He let go of my shoulders and turned away. Suddenly he looked more sad than angry. "That was what he was going to say, that he'd have stopped them if he could because he hated Jason so. But that's not what happened. What happened was that he was caught red-handed helping them—and himself.

I saw Kurt turn toward me, his face white and blind. He suddenly looked so old. I darted through the gate and up to him. "Kurt . . ." I began.

Blue eyes, no longer sharp and clear, but filmed, ashamed, old eyes looked at me. He sort of shook his head to clear it. I grabbed his hand, called his name. At last, he seemed to see me.

"Go away, Rob," he croaked. "Get home. Just go away. Now!"

Mr. Fosse's voice rose again. "Prosecute? Bring charges? You bet I will! I trusted Kurt Doyle with everything I had. I'm going to make sure he rots with his friends!"

There was a chuckle behind me in the dark. I'd forgotten all about Pa. "See?" Pa was saying, soft, "I told you. Everybody is on the take."

I looked at Pa. I looked at Kurt. Then I turned and ran into the dark, ran away from both of them.

CHAPTER 13

You can't keep running forever. Sooner or later, the muscles in your legs cramp up, your lungs can't handle breathing any more, and you fall. About a mile from Fosse's warehouse, I dropped to my knees, gasping for breath. I still could hear Pa's laughter, see Kurt Doyle's eyes.

It wasn't possible. Doyle couldn't have done what Mr. Fosse said. He couldn't have opened that gate for Jason and his thieving crew! He hated Jason worse than anything that crawled on the earth.

"It's not true!" I sobbed in my throat. Yet, if it had all been some kind of mixup, why hadn't Doyle defended himself in front of Mr. Fosse and the police? In front of me and Pa?

In front of Pa! I banged my head on the concrete road, and the pain made me cry out. "Why?" I moaned. Why in front of Pa? I'd wanted Pa to see Doyle, and, yeah, I'd wanted to show Doyle off. Here, Pa, is the father I should have had. I trust this man and I really like him. See, he's never lied to me, not once.

But this time he'd lied. He'd lied, all right! I pictured Doyle in jail with Jason and wanted to throw up. I shook my head to get rid of the picture, but my brain whispered, jail, jail, jail, until I felt numb. I knew I should go back to that warehouse and be with Doyle, but I couldn't make myself do that. Anyway, he'd sent me away. "Go away—you!" that's what he said.

"Robby." I stiffened all over at the sound of Pa's voice behind me. He was panting like he could hardly draw another breath. I looked up and saw Pa outlined in the silver light of the half moon. "You took off so quick," Pa was saying. "I couldn't keep up with you."

"Please," I said, "Please leave it, Pa. Don't say anything." But, of course, he did.

"So that's the kind and generous Kurt Doyle." Even though he was breathless, he was laughing. "A man as honest as the day is long. A policeman with a heart of gold." He choked on his own laughter and started coughing.

I thought of how Doyle had put his coat around me in the van when we were driving from Boston to Laysner. I remembered his hand on my shoulder, his arms around me when I was on that bad grass. I thought of how I'd seen him just now: aged, sagging, afraid.

I felt sick as Pa went on. "At least I didn't ever pretend. I'm what I am. Him? Huh!" His scorn was like a foot in my back, shoving me into the dirt. "Thought he was some kind of angel, did you? Look what he's done!"

"Go away, Pa," I moaned.

I felt his thick hands on my shoulder, turning me around so I had to face him. "Boy, you don't mean what you said just now." In the moonlight, he wore a smug look. "There's a reason for my coming back," he was saying. "That reason is to care for you. We're flesh and blood, and you're like me in many ways. We'll go on together after this, and bygones will be bygones." His eyes glinted. "You're nearly grown. We'll have some fine times, Rob."

Go with Pa? The thought stirred dully in my mind. I wanted to laugh in his face. My place wasn't with Pa anymore. I had a home with Doyle. I started to say this, but the words stuck in my windpipe.

"Go on," Pa said, "spit it out. You want to go back to Mr. Good-Guy Doyle, huh? Well, you can't. Those do-good social workers won't let you live with a convicted criminal."

I felt like he'd dumped a bucket of ice water on me. "You're crazy," I said.

He shook me hard, and this time I didn't even try to break his grip. "You watch your mouth, boy!" he snarled. His hand dived into his pocket and pulled out a bottle. "Here," he said. "You've had a tough evening. This'll cure what hurts you."

He let go of me to uncork the bottle and waved it under my nose. The smell of raw alcohol sickened me. "I thought you were on the wagon."

He laughed. "You go on, now, take a sip," he urged.

He pushed the bottle toward me. His other hand gripped my shoulder, hard. Why not? My tired brain asked. He'll make me, anyway.

"Go on, you little creep, or I'll brain you," Pa muttered.

I set my mouth around the bottle mouth and swallowed hard. Fire shot through me, and my stomach heaved. I swallowed again.

"Now, that's my good boy," Pa purred. It came to me that this was the first time he'd ever said anything nice to me. He liked what I was doing. "You've got stuff in you," Pa went on, in the same pleased voice. "A chip off the old block."

Sirens sounded again in back of us and lights whirred. One, two, three patrol cars whooshed past us. Were they taking Doyle away to the Laysner station to be booked and locked up?

"Nah," Pa said, reading my mind. "They'll let him go. Cops are as thick as thieves. They'll slap his wrists and set him free. We don't have much time, Robby." He took the bottle from me and took a big swallow. "We've got to get going."

Time for what? I wondered. The alcohol was spreading, seeping into the edges of my brain. "Where're we going, Pa?" I slurred.

"To your buddy Kurt Doyle's house, of course! Got to pick up your clothes and what cash we can get our hands on."

"No," I said, and Pa shook me a second time. "We can't steal from Kurt, Pa," I whimpered.

Pa growled that Doyle seemed to be stealing from everybody else. "Of course he stole!" he told me. "Now we're going to help ourselves to what he stole from other folks. We've got to hurry before they turn him loose."

We were walking toward town now. I weaved a

little on my feet, but my mind was clear. I didn't want to go with Pa. I didn't want to leave Laysner. I knew I should shake Pa's hand off and run down the road away from him, but I didn't have the energy. It was like I'd been sick a long, long time. I had no strength left in my legs.

"You do what I tell you, and we'll live easy," Pa said softly. "You mess me up, and I'll beat you so bad you'll forget your own name."

But I knew my name, had always known it. I was Nobody. Doyle had tried to make me into something I was not and never could be. I was Nobody, and Pa's blood was in me, Pa's filthy blood. Now I knew what he meant when he said I could never wash the stink away.

"Nice town," Pa was saying.

We were walking through the town, past the postage-stamp village green and tall white-spired church, past Carmody's darkened store, past the post office and the shops. Everything was quiet except down at the police station.

"Bet they haven't had action like this in years," Pa said, amused. He shoved me into walking quicker. Under the light of Carmody's store I saw that hand—dirty, veined, mottled, disgusting. My skin crawled. I knew the shape of my days if I went with Pa. Drunk or sick, mean or sober, I'd soon be like him. And did that even matter? Pa shoved me again.

"Hurry up," he hissed. "Don't you worry about that Doyle. Cops! Always hassling innocent people. How many times have we been hassled by cops, huh? Well, now they've caught one of their own."

We passed Main and walked onto Peach Street. Pa looked from side to side, approving the neighborhood. "You're lucky, living in a place like this, while I sleep in places they should keep pigs in." He grunted. "Where's Doyle's house?"

It was a stone's throw away. I thought of the first time I'd seen it, heard Elmer bark. He was barking now, an excited whuff-whuff-whuff sound in the night. "That danged dog," Pa said. "I'll shut him up for sure."

"No! I'll take care of it." Pa mustn't hurt Elmer. And how could I take him into Doyle's house? I couldn't! "Pa," I said, "I can't."

He pushed his face close to mine. The veins were standing out in his forehead. His eyes were mean. He pulled back his fist. A squad car turned the corner of the street and slid down the road toward us. Pa let go of me, dropped his hand. The prowl car stopped in front of Doyle's house. And then Doyle got out.

He was okay! He was cleared and they'd let him go! Joy leaped into my throat and I nearly sang Doyle's name out . . . until I saw the way his shoulders slumped. He walked like an old, beaten man.

Pa was the one who spoke. He pushed past me and walked over to Doyle, who was climbing the porch steps. "Mr. Doyle?" Pa said.

Doyle turned, real slow, like a turtle moving its head toward a noise. He didn't say a word, but he saw Pa, and then he saw me.

"You don't know me from Adam," Pa purred. "I'm passing through and I come to see how my boy, Rob, was doing."

"Rob," Doyle said, his voice thick, like he was half asleep. He pulled back his shoulders and really looked at Pa. "You're Rob's father?"

"I am," Pa said, reacting to the returning crispness in Doyle's voice. "I came to see Robby." He grinned, shuffled his feet. "I'd appreciate a place to stay, and food, too."

"You'd settle for money, though." Doyle's voice was exhausted. He reached into his pocket, pulled out his wallet, drew out some bills. "Here's sixty dollars. It's all I have, so there's no use asking for more. You've seen Rob. I think that's all you've come for."

Pa snatched the money, ruffled it between his fingers. "Don't know about that," he said, cunningly. "Don't know. You're in trouble. Maybe I should just take my son with me, huh?"

I thought Doyle would hit Pa. His fist came up, clenched. But he dropped it. "You try and touch that boy," he said, "and I'll have the Department of Social Services and every court in the state after you!" This time, it was his old voice—hard, driving, angry. Pa stepped backwards. "Get out of here, and don't come back!"

Pa didn't even look at me. He stuffed the money into his pants pocket and headed down the road. Then he stopped and turned, lifting his voice. "Yes, *sir!* You listen to me, you no-account trash, Doyle! You're a crook! No matter what you say, you're a crook! And you think you're better than me?"

Lights were going on in houses around us. Dogs started to join Elmer in barking. *Do* something, I thought. Doyle, shut him up! But he only turned slowly toward the door, opened it, and went inside. He didn't look at me, either. I glanced at Pa, who was still yelling, then at the door. Good-bye, Pa, I thought, and hurried into the house after Doyle. It was dark in there. Doyle hadn't turned on any lights. I stumbled up against Elmer, hushed him, and flicked on the kitchen light switch. Doyle was sitting in a chair, slumped over the table.

"You okay?" I asked. He didn't move. Suddenly I got worried about his heart.

I started to go over to him, but he lifted his head and looked at me. His blue eyes were sort of filmed over, the kind of film you see in baby cats and puppies when they are just born. "You okay, Kurt?" I asked again.

He said, "I really messed up, Rob."

I was starting to shake. Elmer came and sniffled at me, so I got down on my knees and held him tight.

"They're saying I'm a crook," Doyle went on in a whispery voice. "They say I'm a crook together with Jason and Seth and Dan. They say I was in with them . . ."

"They're wrong," I whispered, my throat tight. "I know they're wrong. Listen, we can . . ."

He held up a hand, stopped me. "No," he said, "they're right. I did plan this one, Rob. I *was* in on it!"

CHAPTER 14

Outside, Pa had quit his shouting and had gone away. It was suddenly very quiet in the house.

"Yes, I planned it," Doyle told me in that same tired voice. "I got the idea when Seth Boudine came nosing around a few days ago trying to get information on that shipment of electronic games. I knew right away that Jason had sent him, that Jason wanted to get his hands on that shipment. So, instead of throwing Seth out, I talked to him. I got him good and interested and even hinted that I might leave the gate open if the deal was sweet enough."

Elmer was licking my ear. I let go of him, stood up slowly, and looked down at Doyle's bent, white head.

"Rob, I meant it as a trap," Doyle said. "I wanted Jason so bad that I forgot every rule I'd learned on the force." His hands knotted into fists. "I wanted to catch him red-handed so he couldn't wriggle out of it. I wanted to bait a trap for Jason."

My throat was dry. "Why didn't you tell me? Why didn't you say something?"

"Because you might have spoiled the trap. You might have said something in school that could have tipped Seth or Dan off. I don't know." He sighed deeply. "Anyway, I'm glad you weren't involved, because if you were, you'd be in the same mess as me. If that cruiser hadn't come by, I'd have had him, Rob."

"They'll believe you if you tell them," I whispered. "They'll believe you weren't . . . weren't on the take."

"Maybe." He roused himself and sort of nodded toward the hallway. "It's late. We can talk in the morning. Right now, I need to get some sleep."

My legs felt heavy as I walked to my room. Pa's voice started up in my brain. *So he says he planned the whole thing and it backfired. Are you stupid enough to believe him?*

I believed what Doyle told me. I believed him.

How do you know? Pa's voice kept on. *He's using you, Rob. He's always used you. He got money for you from the DSS, didn't he? He made you work cleaning his messy house. He used you so's the townspeople would look up at him and say, "There goes that good, kind Kurt Doyle. Isn't it wonderful what he's doing for that poor kid?"*

"Go away," I muttered out loud.

You're nuts. Pa baited me. *He's lying now, using you. Know how? He'll tell the jury that he did it all for you—did it because Jason gave you the grass that night at the marina. And the bleeding hearts will feel sorry for you and let him go.*

"Shut up!"

Everyone who's ever known you has used you,

Robby, including m e. Me, most of all. Only, I never lied, did I? Doyle lied.

"Are you talking to yourself?" Doyle's voice asked behind me.

I turned quickly, half-shamed but glad that Pa's voice was fading away. "I'm going to bed," I said.

He didn't budge. "I want you to know one thing, Rob," he said. "This was all wrong and it backfired, but in a way I did it for you."

The words bounced across my mind and I heard Pa's faraway laughter. "Don't say it," I begged Doyle.

He got a little red in the face. "I hated what Jason was doing to you. He was the source of that grass you had that night. That's why I did this crazy thing."

"I don't think you did it for me." My voice sounded jerky. "I think you did it for yourself. You hated him because of Alma, didn't you?"

His eyes went narrow, sharp and angry. "You don't know anything about that," he snapped.

"I think I can guess. Seth told me that Alma and Jason were buddies one time. Did he give *her* bad grass?" Doyle's face had gone brick red, but I didn't care. "You blew up at her, and she left your house. You blamed Jason for that instead of blaming yourself."

"That's enough!" he roared.

I yelled back. "Okay, you did me a favor, but that doesn't give you the right to use me."

He smacked me in the mouth. It hurt worse than Pa's hardest blow. For a second we stared at each other, and then Doyle turned white, like all his blood had drained away. "Rob—" he held his hand toward me. I backed away. He dropped the hand and walked out of the room.

I slammed the door after him. I hated him. Pa was right. Doyle was using me now—using me as an excuse. He was like Pa. I remembered how Pa had taken money tonight to go away. And he'd never even said good-bye to me.

"Who needs you?" I mumbled, but, as if the words were a signal, the old, ugly loneliness flooded into me. I began to cry. I threw myself down on the bed and let the tears come. And I swore to myself that I'd never let Doyle or anybody else use me or hurt me again.

I didn't go to school the next day. Doyle wasn't around when I woke up, which was fine by me, and so I just made some coffee for myself and cinnamon toast for Elmer. While he was eating and I was drinking, I heard the van outside. In a while Doyle walked in. He was dressed like I'd never seen him dressed, in suit and tie.

He looked at my coffee mug. "You should have some breakfast," he told me. "Caffeine isn't good for you—or so you say. Don't you practice what you preach?"

Don't you? I thought it, but I didn't say it. I didn't want to say a word to him. He looked across the table at me. "Rob, I shouldn't have hit you last night. I didn't mean to do it. I never would have, except that what you said was cruel, and I lost control." He stood there in his suit, twisting his tie between his fingers. "We need to do some talking, son."

I'm no son of yours, I thought, but again I didn't say it. He sat down at the table. "I was downtown seeing my lawyer. There's going to be an investigation, and then it will go to the Grand Jury to see if there's a case strong enough to go to trial. If the case does go to trial, I have a good chance—my years on the force, my life till now. But I can't prove that I wasn't in on it with Jason and the others. It's their word against mine."

"No one will believe those three," I said reluctantly.

He sighed. "I opened the gate for them. There's no getting around that. And they did have the stuff in their hands." He pounded the table with his fist. "I wish that patrol car had come just a few minutes later! I was just getting ready to arrest them . . ."

I thought of Mr. Fosse's face. He'd been pretty mad last night, but even so he told it the way he saw it. He thought Doyle was guilty. No one would really trust Doyle again. I fingered the place where he hit me. Would *I* trust Doyle?

"That's not the big problem, Rob. Mrs. Towers called while you were sleeping. If I'm convicted, she'll have no choice but to take you away. She's supposed to take you away right now, but there aren't enough homes for adolescent boys, so she won't move that fast."

Elmer nudged my knee, looking for more cinnamon toast. His big, loving eyes made me want to cry. "So what do I do about it?" I asked. And then, something cruel in me made me ask, "What makes you think I'd want to stay here?"

He pulled his tie again. "Nothing," he said. He repeated it. "Neither of us wanted to be stuck with the other, at first. Remember? Only, we became friends, or so I thought." He didn't look at me. "Rosemary did say one thing. When you turn sixteen you can go before Family Court and ask to be declared a major. That means, you can choose whoever you want to live with."

I wanted to go and hug him. Knew I should do that. Knew it . . . and sat there.

"Rob," he said, "don't let my mistake bury us both. Don't let it spoil what you have going for you."

Then he walked down the hall, away from me.

CHAPTER 15

When I went back to school, everyone knew about Doyle's being involved in the warehouse robbery. At first, I hadn't planned on going back to school at all. But Doyle was home almost all day, every day, and I didn't want to be where he was. He didn't sail the boat or do anything, just sat, staring out the window, looking real old and sad. I figured school would be better, but it wasn't.

The news had hit small-town Laysner like a bomb. It began at the bus stop where kids either said, "Hi," and turned to their books, or totally ignored me. I kept looking for Debbie, hoping and dreading I'd see her, but she never did come, and all the other kids pointedly took seats away from me. At the last minute, though, Dan came bouncing up onto the bus. His face flushed with running, he plunked himself down on the seat next to mine.

"They busted Jason," he told me. "He's in jail. Couldn't raise bail money."

"I heard," I said, wishing Dan would keep his voice

down. The kids who'd ignored me had big ears tuned to hear.

"Can you beat that? Old Jason in jail! Seth's father beat the everlasting out of him—that's why he hasn't been in school!" He paused. "Kurt's the smart one. He'll wiggle out of the rap."

I hated Dan. "Maybe he didn't do anything," I said.

"Give me a break," Dan scoffed. "I was right there when he said he might want to be in on the deal. He just wasn't smart, getting caught." He punched my arm. "If he was trying to catch us like he said, why didn't he tell the Laysner cops about us coming there that night. Huh?"

Inside school, it wasn't any better. Kids in the corridors glanced away. Others snickered as I passed. My first period, in Fitz's room, started out okay, though. Mr. Fitz looked at me and greeted me like I was no different than when he'd seen me last. "You've got some catching up to do, Rob," he said in his usual way. "You were out a couple of days, weren't you?"

Someone snickered, and I felt my face grow hot. "Cut that out," I said sharply.

"Oh, better cut it out fast! Otherwise Rob will tell Sergeant Doyle." The kids started to laugh, but Mr. Fitz said, in a voice I'd never heard him use even on Seth, to shut mouths or get out. Then there was a real silence, but I couldn't work.

Next class was English. Mr. Lind greeted me like Fitz had done and told me the assignments I'd missed. He was really nice about it, so, I thought, maybe I'll survive today. But halfway through the period, someone passed me a note. It said "How big a cut did Kurt Doyle give you, Rob?"

Everything went red for a second, then black. Without knowing it, I was on my feet. "Who sent this?" I shouted.

I caught a glimpse of Mr. Lind's startled face, the kids all staring at me, some sympathetically, some laughing, some disgusted.

"Rob, sit down . . ." Mr. Lind began, and then the whisper came from someplace in the room.

"Did Kurt Doyle give you a cut, Ro-beee?"

"Shut up or I'll tear your head off!" I screamed. In the back of the room, a big kid got to his feet.

"Fight!" a guy shouted. I started to run toward the kid, but Mr. Lind was quick for an old guy. He got me around the waist with both arms and hauled me back. He was shouting something, but I couldn't hear him. What I did hear, over and over, was that sneering voice. "I'll take his head off," I shouted.

"Rob!" Mr. Lind snapped. He shook me. "Rob! I can't allow you to act like this in my class, no matter how bad the provocation. Both you and Jim get down to the office, now! I'll let the principal know you're on your way."

I didn't feel hot with rage any more, I felt cold. I was starting to shake, so hard my bones seemed to crush each other. Mr. Lind gave me this sad look. "Rob, later when you've calmed down, come to see me," he said quietly.

Sure, I thought, and I wanted to laugh. Sure, I'd come see him! For what? A lecture? The kid, Jim, glanced at me as we went into the hall. "Hey, you'd better quit being so sensitive," he said. "Why be mad at me? I didn't rob a warehouse."

"Shut up."

"Old holier-than-thou Doyle," he goaded me. "You were his little angel, right? You got caught with your hand in the cookie jar too, I bet."

I should have fought him, but I was shaking so hard. He was big, and he could hurt me, and I was scared. Scared and hating. Why should I fight to clear Doyle's name? I asked myself. The walls of the school seemed to be closing in around me like a trap.

I stopped where I was. To hell with their dumb rules! I wasn't going to the office. I was going home.

I started to turn, but stopped. Doyle was at home. And anyway, it wasn't my home.

"Damn you," I whispered out loud. "Oh, damn you, Kurt Doyle!"

I turned down the hallway and, instead of going to the office, went to my locker instead. I'd take my stuff and leave, anyway. Maybe go down to the beach . . .

"Robby?"

I turned at the sound of Debbie's voice. She was standing a little distance from me, books spilling out of her arms. There was something so good about seeing her—I mean, after this whole foul morning—that a warmth started inside me. It was like the sun had just come up for me. I started to walk toward her, and then the look in her eyes stopped me.

"Deb?" I said uncertainly.

"You lied to me," she said then.

I couldn't say a word. Her eyes were so angry, almost all green, and her mouth was hard. She looked a little like old man Carmody. "You told me lies about your father, Rob! The whole town saw him with you up at the warehouse and, later, he was making a big row up on Peach Street. My father told me. So he had TB, huh? More like the DT's!"

I glared at her. "Listen, I've had enough . . ."

"You've had enough?" She was so mad she was sputtering. "Let me tell you! I told Dad about your pa. Yes, I did. I did it to make him understand and accept you."

"You needn't have done any favors for me. If he can't accept me, he can go to hell," I shouted at her. "So can you!"

I turned on my heel and started to run away from her, but she called me again. This time, she still looked mad, but she looked worried, too. "Where are you going?" she asked.

"What do you care?" I snarled.

"I know where you're going. You're running away. Aren't you? Kurt Doyle is in trouble, and you're going to run away. You're turning your back on him. That's all you can do for your friends!"

"Debbie, if you don't shut up . . ."

"Everyone is talking about Doyle, so you're going to dump him. Now I know you're like your father," she said furiously.

Who are you? I wanted to shout at her. A shrink? How do you know anything about how it is? You have a family, friends. Suddenly I thought, I have to get out of here.

I left the stuff in my locker, beat it to a side door, and went outside. It was cloudy outside, and it was pretty windy, too. Rain had been forecast for later that day, and high winds. It would be windy out on the bay.

I wanted to be free of the land—running free! I hesitated. Could I? Should I? If I went back to the house for the sail, wouldn't Doyle ask me why I wasn't in school, ask me a hundred other dumb questions?

Not if he didn't see me, I argued with myself. Not if I snuck into the garage, took the stuff, and went down to the marina without his setting eyes on me.

"I'll do it," I said aloud. The anger and hurt inside me seemed to still to a kind of waiting. Once out there on the water, I'd be rid of all the feelings and all my problems, if only for a little while.

It wasn't hard getting the sail or trudging the two miles to Peach Street and the two miles back to the marina. It was harder getting the *Dragonfly* ready to sail. There was more wind than I'd realized—it came scudding out of the Atlantic and made the water of the bay choppy and irritable. Good, I thought. It was going to take very bit of my concentration to keep moving without capsizing.

And for sure, that was true! From the first minutes after I got her into the bay, the *Dragonfly* fought me like a bucking horse. She didn't want to sail a true course. She kept turning into the eye of the wind and stopping dead, or else luffing as the wind changed direction on us. I played it cool, though, keeping my eye on the masthead fly, the triangular cloth pennant on the top of the mast. I tried to second-guess the wind and outwit it.

After a while, I got the hang of sailing in the heavy weather, and the *Dragonfly* ran free. She skimmed the water at speeds I hadn't touched before, either soloing or with Doyle. The thought came to me that if he could see me, the old man would be proud. But I bit down on the thought, tearing it away. How did I know if he ever had been proud of me? Maybe it was just an act. Maybe he'd always planned to use me.

To quit thinking of Doyle, I looked up. Heavy gray clouds hung in the sullen sky, and I knew there'd be a good one coming up. This morning, the sun had been blood red. Doyle had taught me enough sailor lore so I knew that meant a warning out in the sea. Well, so be it! I'd sail in a storm. A reckless courage built up in me as I thought of pitting myself against a storm—not the kind of flash storm Debbie and I'd been caught in, but a slow, steady-building one that could be a lot more frightening.

"I don't care, do you hear me?" I shouted at the sky. I *wanted* to be caught in the rain and wind and everything! I wasn't going to sit out a storm safe and snug in the bay.

I glanced at the bottleneck. Under the gray sky, the rocks of the bottleneck seemed blacker than ever. I remembered the big rock shaped like a hand, remembered how cold and slimy it was. I shuddered. Like a dead hand, I thought, reaching out—for me?

For a second I was scared. Then the fear hushed

away. The wind was behind me and I was running free, heading straight toward the bottleneck. I made the *Fly* go faster by lifting the centerboard and shifting the weight into the middle of the boat. The boat rocked up and down on the waves, and I loved it. I laughed and shouted. "I'm not a wimp, I'm not a joke, I'm SuperRob!"

Even when I got to the bottleneck, I wasn't scared. It was hard sailing through it, though. The narrow passageway between the rocks was foaming with angry water that tried to push me back into the bay. I wouldn't buy that. I wished Debbie could see how I put down the centerboard, kept a tight hold on the line, and boldly sailed the *Dragonfly* into the Atlantic.

Right away, there was a change in the water. I could tell that I wasn't in the calm shelter of the bay. For a second, fear came again. Then I was laughing aloud as I played a game with the strong wind and the water. "All right, ocean," I challenged, "amuse me. Show me how good you are."

I ran free, jibed, turned the boat around, and tacked against the wind. I enjoyed the power and the freedom. It didn't matter to me that the sails luffed protestingly against the strengthening wind. I was a match for all of them: Pa, Debbie, Rosemary Towers. Let Towers try to send me to some foster home. If I didn't like where she sent me, I'd take off.

A huge, long gust of wind struck the *Dragonfly.* The whole boat shuddered, then went into the eye of the wind. It stopped. Some of the exhilaration inside me stilled, too. I looked around at the murky gray sea and the angry welts of wild water. The sea seemed to reach for me, curling wet fingers against the hull of the *Dragonfly.*

Suddenly, it stopped being a game. What was I out here for? I asked myself, knowing the answer and not liking it. I was here to finish off what I started on the rooftop in Boston. I'd known then that there'd be another rooftop waiting for me someplace when things got too tough. Here it was, and I'd found it.

A gull flew overhead, mewing in its strange language. I was suddenly cold, and I was scared. Instantly, Pa's voice started in my head. *You're too chicken, Rob, is that it? Realize it! Life is crummy, and you're too dumb, too stupid, to realize that it's best to forget it. End it. Let the sea have you. Just slide over the side, now. It's easier than jumping, and there are no crowds. You'll do yourself a favor.*

A gust of wind caught me and the *Dragonfly,* spinning us around. I tried to steer, but the boat wouldn't obey me. Another gust hit. I knew it was time to take in some sail. Automatically, I lowered part of the main. The gusts came again—much stronger. Wind and salt spray dimmed my eyes. I couldn't see!

That was when the rain started. Rain? It was like a sheet of water that suddenly came into the sky and fell like a gray wall. I could hardly make out the rocks in the bottleneck.

Strangely, I didn't feel any panic. I almost felt relieved. The decision wasn't up to me any more. I could live and make it, or die out here. It wasn't up to me any more. It was up to the wind and the rain and the water. Yet, just as the relief came, it went away. I thought of the small house with the front porch and Elmer begging for his cinnamon toast and the warmth of the kitchen. I saw myself sprawled out on the living-room couch working on an English assignment and Kurt Doyle coming through the door, asking how school had been. I felt the warmth of all that reach out to me. The warmth hurt.

"Stop it," I said. "That's all gone. None of that was ever mine."

My mind threw a few more pictures out. Old Doyle making flapjacks by the stove. The way the sun shone through the drapes in "my" room. Debbie throwing back her hair as we skipped stones in the water.

I didn't want to die!

I wasn't scared to die—but I didn't *want* to! It didn't matter if those warm, good things existed for me or not, I knew they were there. I'd learned what it was to be happy, and that killed everything else. Doyle had showed me what life could be like.

Before, with Pa, I knew nothing could be worse than living. Now I knew life was warmth, and belonging, and loving.

Another gust smashed against the *Dragonfly*. The poor boat groaned. She went into the eye of the wind and stopped, helpless against the pitch of the waves. I'd had no business bringing her out here. I had to take her back! I saw Doyle's face as he'd shown me the *Dragonfly* for the first time. Mad at him or not, I didn't have the right to destroy his boat! But how to get back?

I came about and glanced down at the compass tied to the mast. It was almost too gray to see, but if the compass held true, I should head northwest. I began to tack slowly against the wind, heading toward where I hoped the opening of the bottleneck would be. But the sea pushed me back. It seemed to be laughing at me. The water was playing games with me now, like a cruel cat with a mouse.

We played the game for a while. I refused to give up. I figured that I could maybe ride out the storm where I was. If the rain would just ease up, I'd be able to see the bottleneck and plot my way through it. But the spumes of gray water kept getting worse and worse.

Suddenly I heard the buzz of a motorboat in the distance, above the roar of the storms.

"Rob! Ro-beee!"

Something tightened inside me. That voice! The first thankfulness I'd felt ebbed away. I clung grimly to the reduced sail. The boat pitched and hobbyhorsed as the swells hit it.

"Rob! Are you out there? Rob!"

Why had he come out for me? I asked myself bitterly. To make me beholden to him again?

I didn't want to be rescued by Doyle. I didn't want to be in his debt again. I didn't want to start feeling for him the way I'd started feeling. He wasn't going to hurt me again if I could help it.

The motorboat roared closer. Now I could see its yellow eye. "Robby . . ." Doyle shouted. I knew he'd spotted me. He was shouting, but most of the words got lost in the wind. "I have a line!" I heard him yell. "Make it tight to the *Dragonfly*'s mast and come aboard!"

"No!" I yelled.

"Rob, make sense!" His voice was coming ragged against the storm. Under me the *Dragonfly* pitched and pleaded, Please! Take me home! I gritted my teeth. A wave smashed against the bow, filling my eyes and nose and mouth with spume. "The storm is going to get worse. The weather report . . ." I didn't get what the weather report was, but Doyle's voice came back. "I don't know if we can even navigate the motorboat through the bottleneck. Hurry!"

I heard a snap of sound. The jib had come unfastened. It was flapping up, out into the strong wind and catching it. The *Dragonfly* veered crazily. I fought down the jib, tried to secure it against the lurching boat.

"Rob, get the line! Listen . . . me!" Doyle's voice was desperate.

A thick line flew through the air and fell short. The *Dragonfly* began to dig its nose into the water. It was no use! I'd have to make it back with Kurt Doyle. I'd figure out later what I owed, what I didn't owe.

"I'm throwing the line again!" His words were sliced off by a wail of wind. "Rob, the line . . ."

I'm not sure what happened next, except that as the line came through the air, Doyle moved. He'd been this dark shape on the motorboat till now. Now his shadow moved. Maybe he came to the edge of the boat so the line wouldn't fall short. One moment he was on the deck of the motorboat. Then he was down on his knees.

I shouted his name. What was wrong with him? "Kurt!" I yelled. A huge wave came smashing against the *Dragonfly*'s bow, drowning both boat and me. I spluttered through it, fought to pull the *Dragonfly* closer to the motorboat, and lost sight of Doyle. When I could see again, I stared hard.

Doyle was buckling, falling forward, toppling into the white water . . .

CHAPTER 16

"Kurt!"

I let go of the tiller, clung to the pitching side of the *Dragonfly,* stared at the crazy, dark water. Then I saw Kurt Doyle's orange lifejacket. And one white hand, clawing, reaching out over the water.

Instinctively, I grabbed the rope around the mast and tied a knot around myself. I jumped into the water. It was cold. The shock drove the air out of me. I gasped and gulped fast breaths, felt light-headed. I can't hyperventilate, I thought. Doyle had warned me . . .

Where *was* he? I screamed his name. A smack of cold water stifled me. The waves looked like mountains. I couldn't see anything except the valleys in the water.

"Kurt!" I yelled again, but all I got was a mouthful of brine. I tried to crest the waves, my lifejacket helping me to bob around. Where was he? I panicked. Where *was* he?

Then I saw him bobbing a little way to the left. His jacket was buoying him up. He lay in a dead man's float, face in the water, suspended on the waves. He looked as if . . .

"No!" I sobbed.

I lunged toward the limp form in the water, desperately thrashing to get to him. The ocean pushed me back. A swell as big as a small mountain cut us off.

Please, I thought, oh, please! Salt water filled my mouth and ears and eyes. With both hands I tried to push the hateful dark water away. I felt the hard tug of the rope around my waist. The *Dragonfly* was tugging me away from Doyle. The boat was stronger than I was. It was being pulled by the storm currents.

What could I do? Loosen the rope? But what would happen when I reached Doyle?

Just then the orange of Doyle's lifejacket bobbed toward me. The same current that was carrying the *Dragonfly* away was bringing Doyle closer. Sobbing, I lunged for him. My fingers felt icy and numb and almost useless. I hooked them into the edge of his lifejacket and hung on. Hanging onto that lifejacket was the hardest thing I'd ever done in my life. I hauled Doyle's inert form closer and tried to push my legs under his, but I couldn't.

I called his name. He didn't hear me. No use trying to talk. I pulled his head back out of the water. His eyes were closed, his mouth working. There was pain written all over his gray face. I had to get him back to the motorboat!

I looked where the motorboat should be. My heart truly stopped. The boat was about a hundred yards away! I could see its yellow eye gleaming through the grayness. The light was far, far away.

Another tug at my waist—the *Dragonfly,* too, was anxious to be gone. Suppose the rope parted? I gritted my teeth and started to swim, dragging Doyle with me. He hung lifeless in the water beside me. A swell broke over our faces. I saw the trickle of saliva at the corner of his slack jaw. What was wrong with him? Had he hurt himself falling off the motorboat? Somehow, though, he'd seemed sick before he fell.

Inside my head, I knew. Heart. But I tried not to think, tried to keep swimming. I wasn't a bad swimmer, but those heavy seas were punishing. Each breath I drew was like a battle. I was sobbing and gasping for air. Every time I gained a few feet, the *Dragonfly* pitched away. The rain came heavier, too, driving, drumming . . .

"Kurt, help me," I gritted. "Try to help me . . ."

Then I groaned. The jib of the *Dragonfly* had broken free again. It started to belly out. If the sail caught the wind, there was no way we could catch up! It wouldn't stay afloat long on these waters. It would capsize or crash against the rocks!

I grabbed the rope and started to pull myself, one-handed, toward the boat. I was exhausted. I was starting to hyperventilate again. No use, I thought.

"Robby." His whisper was so soft I couldn't hear it. I felt it, rather, coming from those rubbery, gray lips. "Get . . . out," Doyle was telling me. "Leave . . . me!"

He wasn't dead! Exultation swept through me, gave me the last push I needed to grab the edge of the boat.

I clung to it. I had it . . . now what? I looked at Doyle. If I lifted him into the boat, it would tip.

Doyle gave some kind of moan with words in it. "Hang . . . on this side."

Hang on. Meaning to keep going? I groaned. A wind struck the boat, turning it around, nearly making me lose hold. I glanced at Doyle, praying he was still okay. His hands were weakly grabbing for the side of the boat.

Suddenly I understood! He wanted to balance the boat. Hadn't he taught me about balance? That was why you hiked out, to balance the boat! Doyle wanted to hang onto this side of the boat and balance it so that I could swim to the other side and climb in! Even in these rough seas, it might work! But suppose he didn't have the strength to hold on?

"Only . . . way," he gasped.

His big, stubby hands closed on the edge of the boat. His face was a blur of pain. I tried to untie the rope from my waist, tie it around him, but my fingers were numb. The knot wouldn't give. I sobbed.

". . . time," Doyle said. No, there was no time!

I gave him a despairing look and left him. Hold on, I thought, prayed, begged, as I half-swam, half-groped my way around the hull. Hang on! I was sobbing, begging, pleading, as the waves smashed against me and the water crested over my head. Hold on . . .

I was on the other side. The boat pitched and heeled. I pulled myself up, then collapsed at the bottom of the boat. I crawled across and reached for Doyle. If he'd given up, if he wasn't there . . .

But he was. I grabbed his arms and heaved. He

didn't help. He went limp, a deadweight. I cried as I hauled him in. He collapsed at the bottom of the boat, not spread out flat, but curled with arms across his chest. Around his heart.

I bent over him. "Kurt . . . how bad?" I sobbed.

His lips were gray. He twitched them like he wanted to smile and couldn't. Nothing in my whole life hurt me like his trying to smile. I had to get him some help, fast. But how?

I looked around wildly for an answer. Then I screamed out loud. Looming out of the grayness ahead was that huge rock hand! It was reaching for us, reaching—

I jumped backward, leaned hard on the tiller, and grabbed for the loose jib. It danced madly, flapping out as I leaned, pressed, bore down on the tiller. On a shriek of wind, with an awful, scraping sound, the boat slid clear of the big rock hand.

"What do I do, Kurt?" I cried.

I knew what had to be done, but now that I'd cleared the big rock hand, I couldn't see it, nor any of the slimy waiting rocks of the bottleneck.

Think, I told myself. Think! I banged my fist against my forehead. I put it to my mouth and bit the knuckles. Think!

"I have to sail through the bottleneck, Kurt," I finally said out loud like he could hear. "It's the only way!"

I secured the jib. My fingers were so numb and useless I had to battle with the rope for a few minutes. Then I glanced down at Doyle, looked at the compass, and pushed the tiller. I began to guide the boat toward the big, black, rock hand.

I couldn't see it. Couldn't see it. Couldn't— "There it is!" I yelled.

It rose above me more like a hand than ever. I could see the sea spray spuming off it, and the dead men's knuckles rising out of the dark water to grip me. I ground my teeth as I tried to steer, then grabbed an oar and started to row like mad. Wind turned the boat again. I rowed and steered.

Was the wind stronger? I didn't know. I didn't dare look at the sky, but I knew huge rolls of cloud were up there. They had more rain stored in them, more rain and wind and storm. I said a prayer, pushed the tiller.

Scrape. Thud. The rock reached for us, got the hull of the boat. "No!" I screamed, and then, with a gust of wind, we were by. I looked back, unbelieving. I escaped the big stone hand!

"Kurt! We did it!" He was lying on the bottom of the *Dragonfly,* and he hadn't moved. Was he dead already? I started to cry, but I dashed the tears away.

There was no time to cry. Another rock rose dead ahead of us.

I tried to map out the rocky bottleneck in my mind, to remember exactly how I'd sailed through all those times with Doyle, and then by myself. The biggest rocks should be coming on the port side, I hoped.

Sailing and paddling and steering blind, I guided the boat as best as I could. She hardly obeyed me, for the storm was very strong now. Again, there was the scraping of rock on the bottom of the boat.

"We're past another one, Kurt!"

I was too scared to think of being afraid. "There have to be some more rocks to starboard. I wish we could see them, Kurt. Hard enough steering, but not seeing is worse."

A huge wave smashed into us, blinding me. The *Dragonfly* hobbyhorsed. When the water cleared from my eyes, I saw darkness ahead. Darkness of rock or storm? I wondered. Into my mind rushed that familiar, sneering voice.

You little creep. It's your fault, you know that? You walked away from this man because you were too stupid to see that he loved you. Now he's dying because of you. Why keep trying?

I didn't even tell the voice to go away. Why? It was not Pa's voice, never had been. It was my own voice, coming from that part of me that was like Pa, that part of me that had given up and wanted to die.

"I have to get Kurt back!" I sobbed.

As if in answer, the winds eased for a fraction of a second. The rain seemed to veer away from me, and I could see—

See the dark rock teeth grinning, just feet away from me!

CHAPTER 17

One more second, and we'd be on those rocks!

The *Dragonfly* was hobbyhorsing wildly. It wanted to be carried onto those rocks, wanted the struggle to be over. "You can't have Kurt!" I screamed.

The jib let loose and fluttered free with a whapping sound. The boat heeled. I hiked out as far as I could go, body half in water. The boat turned, went into the eye of the wind. I glared at the rocks.

"Kurt, hang on. We'll do this somehow!"

I spoke out loud to hear a voice, any voice, something human above the storm sounds. Then I seemed to hear Debbie's voice, reading. Reading that Kipling poem.

" 'If you can force your heart and nerve and sinew . . . to serve your turn long after they are gone . . .' "

Kipling for skipping. Elmer. The quiet house and the kitchen with the sun pouring in.

"We're going to do it, Kurt!" I said between clenched teeth. The *Dragonfly* veered, hobbyhorsed, and heeled in protest as I began to tack under the jib toward the rocks. The teeth were very close. One wrong gust and we'd be gone.

". . . 'where there is nothing in you,' " Debbie's voice sang to me, " 'except the will that says to you—hold on!' "

I whispered the lines to myself. Over and over. They were no longer a poem I'd had to read for English; they were words living and real. I had to hold on! Even if there wasn't a hope or a chance left.

Crunch! The *Dragonfly* caught the first rock in the bow. The whole of her shuddered. "Hold on, boat!" I yelled at her.

Then, the wind changed.

I could see the sail filling, bellying out. The wind started to push us gently—started to push us through the bottleneck. The wind was my friend, for now. But for how long?

"You taught me, Kurt," I shouted. "You taught me how to sail the bottleneck. I'm not going to let you down! You said I was smart, you said I was good, said you were proud of me!"

The wind shifted. We were halfway through the bottleneck, but it wasn't going to let us through. The rocks were leaning over us, mocking. I tried to come about and tack, but the gale was too strong. The *Dragonfly* bucked. I'd made a mistake.

Everyone made mistakes. Doyle had made one. Doyle had feet of mud, like Pa, like me. The difference was that Pa made mistakes out of greed and meanness. Doyle made his out of love.

Something inside my brain and heart seemed to

slide together, slide into place. Fighting for our lives, half drowned and half frozen, desperate for help, I felt a strange kind of happiness.

"I'm doing the best I can for us, Kurt," I said. "I don't know the answers. You did the best you could for me—or Alma—it doesn't matter any more. You did it because you loved us, that's all that matters." I raised my voice. "Kurt, do you hear me? I love you."

The wind grabbed my words and threw them back into my face. I thought, Please! For Kurt's sake, change. Give me one break. I gritted my teeth, pushed the tiller, and prayed, struggling to push us through those dark teeth.

Was it my imagination? Had the wind dropped a little? I held my breath. Suddenly the rocks were behind us, and the *Dragonfly* was sailing into the open water of the bay. "We got through!" I yelled.

I shouted it again to Doyle. He lay where he was. Terror filled me. Was it too late? Was he dead? I let go of the tiller and threw myself down beside him, grasping one thick wrist. My numb fingers couldn't find a pulse, but when I shoved my ear down to Kurt's chest, I could hear a thready beat. It sounded slow and tired, but he was still with me.

He was having trouble breathing. I pushed back his head, held his nose, took a lungful of air, and poured it into his mouth. Breathe, Kurt, I begged. Hang in there. Don't die.

I breathed deep into him. His eyes stayed closed, his face gray, but it seemed that maybe he was breathing a little easier. Then I felt the wind shift and looked up.

The rocks of the bottleneck rose up just behind us. We were being pushed back against the rocks!

I scrambled to the tiller and tried to steer. The wind had changed its mind and decided to be our enemy again. It was going to make sure Doyle and I died out here. How was I going to get us back to shore in this?

As if in answer to my thought, the sound of a motor came from far away. It was the choking, grunting sound of a motorboat. A flashing light bounced back and forth over the water.

"Kurt, they're coming for us. Help is coming. Please hold on just a little while more!"

CHAPTER 18

The coast guard cutter got Kurt into the motorboat right away. They made me come, too, and tied a rope around the *Dragonfly*'s mast so they could drag her to shore. I was glad. Kurt loved that boat.

Two paramedics had come with the coast guard, and they started working on Doyle right away. They gave him oxygen and began monitoring his vital signs, which they radioed in to a hospital not far from Laysner.

"Will he be okay?" I begged.

They were giving him medication and didn't—couldn't, maybe—answer me. Instead, they wrapped me in a blanket, gave me coffee. "We're going to do everything we can," one of the paramedics told me. "He looks to be a strong man. He proved how tough he was by staying alive all this time. The will to live is important in heart attack cases . . ."

Someone in the cutter told me it was lucky one of the kids noticed the *Dragonfly* gone from the marina and called for help. I figured that was Debbie. She probably called the house and, deciding Doyle had come after me, called the coast guard. I tried to be grateful to Debbie, but she seemed so far away. Everything and everybody—Pa, Debbie, the town—seemed far away. Reality was Kurt and me—and death.

"How is he?" I kept asking.

I sat next to Kurt, not touching him, but watching the rise and fall of his chest, the grayness of his face. I wanted to do something for him. "I didn't ask for you," he had once said to me, and I hadn't asked for him, either, but life, or the hand of Providence, or whatever it was Doyle called it, had given us to each other. I couldn't let Kurt go now.

I reached out and touched his cold hand. "Don't go," I said. I didn't care what happened, as long as Kurt lived. Maybe there would be a trial and things would go badly and Mrs. Towers would take me away. So what? When I was sixteen, I'd come back to Kurt. Then we could be together, go on together. We wouldn't always agree, and that was okay. We'd try, and fail, and get up again and try once more. Trying was what it was all about. If Kurt lived, I'd try again.

And if he died?

I didn't want to think of that. We reached the shore and Kurt was bundled, me right next to him, into a waiting ambulance. What if he died? I asked myself. I didn't know, but I did know one thing: there'd be no more rooftops for me. Kurt had shown me that at the risk of his own life.

"I'm going to try," I whispered to him. "You try, too!"

They wouldn't let me into the emergency room,

where he was taken. They made me wait outside, and some doctor came and bandaged me and put stuff on my cuts and bruises. I asked about Kurt.

"We won't know for a while," he said, sounding real doctor-like. But he seemed to take pity on me, because he put a hand on my shoulder. "You brought him in, son. We'll try to make him okay," he said.

Yes, I had brought him in, but now what? Well, I waited. I don't know how long I waited, but it seemed a long, long time. At last a door opened and another doctor called my name. "Rob Holland?"

My legs were rubbery as I stood up. I felt like I was facing the bottleneck again. "Yes?" I croaked.

He smiled and tension fell away. I felt like fainting in relief. "He's all right? He'll be okay?"

"Not so fast," he said. "He's been in one of the worst storms around, and he's had previous heart trouble. That should have killed him, but willpower can work miracles." He paused. "He wants to see you."

I started to run past him. He grabbed my arm. "He's in the Coronary Care Unit, the CCU, son. It still could go either way. Say nothing to upset him or get him excited. Hear me? And only a few minutes."

I felt scared all over as I followed the doctor down the hall to the CCU. Once inside, I was even more terrified. They had Kurt strapped to all these machines and tubes, and he looked small and white on the hospital cot.

I thought, he's sick, he's really sick, and then I thought of all the things that had happened, would still happen in spite of today. The grand jury. Court, maybe.

And no matter how you sliced it, the loss of his good name . . .

The doctor had said willpower was important. Supposing Kurt decided he didn't want to live with all the mess going on?

I went close to his bed, wanting to throw my arms around him, reassure him, tell him we were a team. I wanted to, but remembered what the doctor had said—no excitement. I looked down at the shrunken white thing that was Kurt, and then I saw his eyes.

They were still clear and sharp. They were the same eyes that had tried to smile through pain. I'm proud of you, the eyes now told me. Told me that, and something else, told me of a worry that had nothing to do with the grand jury or any of that.

I took his hand. The thick fingers were weak and limp. I held them tight. "They won't keep you here too long," I said, my voice husky and strange in my ears. "Whenever they let you out I . . . I want you to come home with me."

For a second, he just looked at me. Then the worried look went away, and he closed his eyes.

"Kurt?" I whispered.

His hand squeezed mine. A promise.